Leodor Bumb: Outward

- Aron Micko H.B

Dedicated to my trash ideas

(1-140 Conceptual Characters)

And to *my friend Miguelito Limbagan "Migs- da MVP"*

(Who wants to help me but he passed away.)

"Farewell, my friend. BTW if you have time there in heaven just read this fiction. Thank you."

The Termination

In the eyes of the selfish ruler, the blue is full of foes and the underworld is the angels fought.

My confidence that I would pass Honolio's tailored test sank.

They're right.

His expectation is different from my hope, believing that I would passed all the trials. I remarked that the only thing I fell for, was his expectation.

Honolio is our master at the Woil West Temple. We are among the majestic first class who are taught to protect and provide stretching rations during the time of shortage for the proletariat or working class below the mountain.

Previously, the desire of my fellow Dotsets is to help people in need of essential things 'a shelter for all folks'. Advantage of living in a mountainous place, we could easily see the whole area however the temple was swallowed by thick fog for all years when we tried to look at the top of the temple.

In the present day, almost all of the Dotsets are accustomed to changing.

Knowing what is happening outside the solid temple, shrouded in darkness and here in the Woil West Temple, I believe we have the key to solving and eliminating the poisonous evil things spreading around the outside.

However no one dared to go out of the temple. When we open the gate and we move our feet to walk out of the shrine it is death that we all afraid. Our Honolio doesn't open anything and let nothing out lightly because caring and protecting us is more way important than any kind of missions.

The saddest thing arrived is that something happened… a crisis result.

 I wholeheartedly affirm that I passed the trial given to me by our Honolio. Honest person and I have admired Honolio since I was a child. I couldn't understand why ... Why I was one of the fatal Dotsets in his trial.

I tried to approach him and ask why it turned

out that way. I just stopped because I saw the

sadness in his eyes and tried to walk a little

towards him but the tears came out of his eyes

even promptly.

Widaway Trial is one of the unacceptable

cultures here in Woil West Temple wherein all of

the Dotsets are compelled to join if you passed

you are safe but if not you will encounter the

providence of vestige life in the husk.

The test is simple, we wait for the result

announced by our Honolio while doing nothing.

The Widaway Trial is a directive order that no one knows who is passed or not unless you are the master of all Dotsets. Only the Honolio knew it.

We witnessed for the first time Honolio's emotion, tears in the eyes of our Master. There was nothing he could do even if I approached him and asked, I knew that this was the end of our lives.

I could see in Honolio's eyes that he was just compelled by what was happening and I didn't know too, what really happened.

Instead of being annoyed with our Honolio, it was replaced by pity.

"I'm sorry," The brief simple word sobbed by our Honolio brought tears in our eyes. Only now did I find him having complications discussing and apologizing to us.

Our Honolio stood up and sauntered directly in front of the students still like me waiting for the result and he went on to speak and mention the failed Dotsets like me.

"Marlen Balas, you're one of my fun and playful Dotsets. Please stand up."

"Legar Velma, sociable. Please stand up."

"Yora Dence, you can-" Our Honolio's words were cut short as that Dotset stood up calmly immediately. Our Honolio just nodded.

"Katho Don, I'm proud of you. Sorry, please stand up."

"Rion Hein, you're one of those who showed loyalty as you helped me cure my illness. I'm sorry, please stand up."

"Sealo Wise, sorry."

"Carrin Regra, I have respect for you. Sorry, please stand up"

"Vidia Ercado, I have nothing to tell you. I'm sorry."

"Brane Yares, thank you so much for your courage and ability. Thank you and I apologize humanly."

Ten of us, I estimated the names mentioned by our Honolio , unlike me, I listened to no word like telling me to stand up.

The mere aspect I heard at initial was that he mentioned my name, I did not only see in the eyes of our Honolio the frustration rather it was sadness and blubbering voice as he spoke of my name that I similarly could not withhold I was caressed by emotion. I moved to rips by not understanding and inferring why I'm included among those who failed to pass his test.

***

My fellow Dotsets who had passed laughed at us, I didn't recognize who; but I heard some of them. When I looked back to find who was cracking up it was back to precisely normal. I remember the fact that we similarly do that, back last year when someone failed like us.

Excluding them is one of the fulfilling acts that I have already done several couples of times. The hate and frustration of becoming better cynical are occasionally shadowing my central nerves, it may be an adverse impact but in some way had the advantage. The aspect is, there's a murky side in my sense as the others, I'm speculating. The Honolio instructs us to satisfy adequately and explore more core in meditations it benefited me a lot in my years of committing what he mocked. But now it's varied.

A substantiated fact of the critical impediment of leaving is here, in our way.

The ten of us facing death. It's a valuable rule in the belief in the ahead years of our staying here in the temple. If someone failed the tests and trials. They need to face the outward life in the temple.

Like we are.

I didn't think it was a punishment for me, it's more than that. An absurd and suicidal mission will unfold after our Honolio's announcement.

As I think when I saw the other students who failed who'd similarly like me. Various emotions and acceptance.

We messed and twisted, by the intractable judgment. The guilty we face is our own mistake. There's nothing to carry our fault, our Honolio didn't do anything but declare the results only. In my deliberation, nothing changed what I've done is not of my Honolio's profession after all. Sadly I will never be one of his students starting today and counting. Our Honolio apologized to us many times even he didn't do anything.

" So now, we are ten." I heard some Skinny older guy failed like me. "How are you, chubby kid?"

"I'd a name, it's Leodor Bumb," I teased him.

"Leodor Bumb, of course it's you Leodor. You can call me Katho Don or Katho or maybe Don if you want." He trailed off to me while lighting-smoking pipe. He introduced his named ever though we already knew each of us.

"Katho, stop it. This is my one hundred twenty four warnings smo-" interrupted Honolio's saying.

"Smoking pipe is prohibited at the Woil West temple." Katho Don continued our Honolio speech. " Yeah, I heard it. But I'm ignoring you."

Our Honolio didn't say anything but he nodded in the bitter way Katho Don says.

"Oh by the way no hurt feelings, Master. It's my last day here, forgive me." Katho Don added to the talk of our Honolio while I'm listening to them.

He has a gut to oppose our Honolio, I can't deny the fact the recklessness of him similarly old like our superior. In the past year until now I never heard Katho call our superior as Honolio. He called our Honolio "Master", different but similar meaning.

Honolio hesitated nothing, it's normal. Being an observer during his lessons I developed to study his Limbic System.

The only thing I failed to predict is the early announcement.

For a failure, we see ourselves no different. The question of the word "Why?" is simple to answer but it's personal for some many cases that we have the emotion of failing to something that we knew it's very hard to forget and the way of my understanding in the crisis we engaged is no different of being a loser. I study precisely to stay by maintaining what should I be supposed to be. In the results of the trials, my confidence fell for something.

The something that I talking about is the negative side. Katho Don sits beside me, I can't say to him that I hate the smoke of his pipe. I distance myself from him pretending that I looked at somewhere. It's a good try but my plan run out in disappointment when he tried to stand up too. The smoke of his pipe chased at me without having any intentions. The annoying fog turns and I hold my breath in seconds. The problem of being not a smoker is obviously on me.

I heard abandoned steps from our Honolio on us. It was not the last but a sign.

On the inside thoughts are like a preparation if I'm speaking to myself but it's unpredictable, he was just like giving us a blessing before we go out in the temple. A little concern is not what I need but a piece of survival advice or some deeper important saying that will uplift what we feel but we hear nothing.

The ten of us waiting for our time. Until we heard the word "Wait" from our Honolio. It's short but a little reasonable cut of words that made us expect in promising without having a second back-conclusion.

Realizing that we are continuing to die makes me easy to refuse to think.

If somebody can unlock the entrance right now, I entirely go there and wait to slathered my blood to ashes.

We wait until we saw Honolio's back, no difference. Nothing new, except now he was holding a pendant.

He looks on us and straight walks in front of me. I thought he will give me the pendant as a remembrance, I'm assuming but it's not happened.

He gave the pendant to my fellow failed Dotset beside me and his name is Marlen Balas.

"Honolio, what's this?" Marlen asked.

"A mission, this is the only thing I can give to all of you. A key to curing the Penac." Honolio replied and I stared at the pendant, we focused see our last hope an important thing to our eye like gold.

"Penac, th-the brutal sickness."Marlen Balas exclaimed.

"Of course, it is, Oldman." Katho Don replied rudely to Marlen Balas.

"Oldman? We were same age idiot." Marlen Balas hissed to Katho Don before the worst conversation began. Honolio snatch the pendant to Marlen Balas and he gave it to me.

"I'm not sure." I grumbled to our Honolio and he gave the pendant to the person next besides Marlen Balas and his name was Legar Velma.

Legar Velma is a friendly student he's no issue with bad behavior to anyone. I think he's more fitted to the task of holding the pendant compare to me.

"Oh, unfair." Marlen Balas replied and our Honolio looks seriously at him, Marlen shut his mouth and nodded.

I agreed when Honolio take back the pendant in my hand and bring it to Legar. I didn't see myself leading them.

Honolio says something to Legar Velma. I didn't know what it is. But after their conversation, Legar Velma acts differently like an active one.

"Alright listen to me." Legar Velma recalled all of us, trying to call our attention. But it seems some of my fellow garbage students ignore him in front.

In my mind I used the word garbage to simply things in life without over explaining how failure we are.

Our Honolio countered, "Thank you, sorry." I looked at him in the eyes, I saw the cries of my teacher and he turned back on us and walked.

 Leaving is another way to forget us.

"Don't cry kid, he's a p*ssy ." Katho Don stated to me. I didn't cry but in my opinion, Honolio gave us hope by giving us the key, a pendant. A reason for a mission to save humanity from Penac. The only way to survive is if we want to survive.

In a minute, the gate will open. No foods or preparations, as the rule of the Woil West Temple. It's hard, a risky act the only thing we have is the Pendant for some guidance. All maps of the world get burned almost in the century, in our place maps didn't exist anymore. We have been here in the Woil West Temple for decades but when it comes to the outside world only ancient books are my basis.

During a lunch break in the temple when I was a kid my favorite spot place is the library.

I saw the book "Endless" in which the trees, plants, and various animals in the outside world of the temple are described in writing and I'm trying to imagine it more, I didn't finish reading the book but it remains something familiar in my memory.

***

Some of them.

Katho Don, Marlen Balas, and Legar Velma hold the lead and I follow them hopefully they're the best team. Four of us and the remaining six, I'm not close to them neither as a colleague nor friend. Knowing them is like I'm wasting my time and emotions if some of us getting killed.

I see ourselves as nothing, however we have value in remaining precarious missions.

***

We heard the alarming admonition sound of the gate. The opening of it makes me think there is a lair. In the book that I read, the forebear Honolio didn't mention a lot of any survival tactics in the outside temple. We are all amateurs. Whether my age is different from some of them, I assure in some way that I need them, we need each other to finish the goal.

The vigilance part of us is progressive.

Except for Yora Dence, he's always calm and unpredicted enigmatic useless, I didn't know him a lot. But people called him stingy for his selfish behavior when he doesn't cooperate with any teamwork. Lack of participation and unfriendly attitude makes him so useless to us.

"Why are you looking at me? Are you gay or what?" Yora Dence added to Carrin Regra, while I'm observing them. I became more perceptive in my surroundings who ever knows, maybe they are the key to my safety.

"Say that to yourself, idiot." Carrin Regra replied and Yora Dence didn't respond.

Carrin Regra got a heroic posture compared to Yora Dence he's a man with honor. He's responsible for all of his commitment, The question remains unfold he didn't pass the trials and tests in our Honolio. Unlike in previous years, I thought he couldn't pass all the trials because he was not prepared and he was ready to die for this tradition but something miraculous happened and the destined work present. The time, he was lucky to pass all and he got an average score results that make him safe. An asset, we need his strength. He can be useful to us compared to Yora Dence.

On my side, I saw Vidia Ercado show his knife he looks like a murderer, a killer waiting for his prey. He caught my attention because he's just like trying to stab some of us first target assuming it is Brane Yares.

"Hey!" Legar Velma noticed it too. "What are you doing?"

"Nothing. Incase." Vidia Ercado replied to Legar Velma and Brane Yares take a look at his back, I know he got confused about what's going on with his back.

Vidia Ercado is a skinny guy. Not actually a threat but he's just a silent killer. Limited knowing what his purpose is but he seems like a blackguard to me. I distance myself in his way. Judging him in case, he looks like a betrayer.

"Alright, listen to me! I'm a leader." Brane Yares snapped to all of us. Everyone was pissed when he talked because he always pondered that he was the leader even though we wouldn't have. A self-proclaim leader but it's more like he's a manipulator. One of my memories when we are students, all the time he claims all the credits of the whole member of his group.

The no merci life begins.

Proving for something useful than staying in the temple makes me feel like a turtle.

No confident only courageous act.

The hell start to dwell.

We are waiting while walking for our time.

Meant for…

Touch-and-go

Disapprove of wrongdoing; Year after year they can't remember the real right doing.

We passed on the gate, stepping in the outside is not hard and typically normal except through the new surroundings that we face. A misty tree and grasses in the moist smell of the down forest, I can determine by smelling the fogs, having experience when I was a kid and it's not dangerous on the outside that time.

I'm naive, just like the ten of us. Some of them are scared, some are just curious, the others didn't care at all.

Inside my firmness of purpose, I confess to myself that some of my members are indecisiveness mind.

There's no resolution of plans only the self-proclaim idiot leader had a plan.

We didn't follow him, instead, we goes where our feet goes. It doesn't matter, gratefully he didn't get the pendant key. I followed the means of state leaders who wear the pendant.

Proceedings to the mordacious mentation to the temple similitude to the outside are no divergence at all.

"Hey kid, follow me." Vidia Ercado ordered to me in his eyes sharp-sightedness.

Vidia Ercado is the type of person that I didn't trust. My perspicacity involved in my mind, on his speech act.

The answer to what I can do right now on Vidia Ercado's invitation attempt is I have options.

Number one: Reject it.

Number two: Accept it and go with him.

Number three: Ignore and pretend that I didn't hear what he put forth.

I evaluate the last pick conclusion, a best part was I consider something like less enough suffering if I reject it.

The two were risky enough to deal with because of his murderer look appearance and it includes the bad impression that I felt when he tried to stab Brane Yares even he's skinny I considered his treason.

I stated the third option as the best. I walked dissembling acted stupidly in locomotion. My manner of walking is different from what I naturally pass over in arrival.

Vidia Ercado goes in a different direction of our mission.

We didn't know about his plan, about his action on why he do it but in some ways, I felt less risk of exposure to the demise.

I count and we are nine, my group didn't manage to deal with what's Vidia Ercado's act.

"The less the better." Sealo Wise quaked to me while walking maybe he find out what was happening in my small communication with Vidia. I tried to check what's noesis about him by asking a question.

"What do you mean?" I asked Sealo Wise what he was talking about, even though I simulated it.

Sealo Wise is a small man and skinny like Vidia Ercado.

But one thing that I can anticipate him compared to Vidia is Sealo was a helpful friend, in the past year there's no any crappy volition or misleading bad subject matter on him, in his earnest he was functional to use in the team even I didn't conceive our group as a team, yet.

"We can't trust him, I saw what you saw. He tried to stab an idiot. " Sealo Wise replied to me with convincing thoughts. I agreed we can't trust Vidia Ercado and I agree when he grumbled the perfect word to Brane Yares.

Walk to the downfield of Woil West temple, The ambiance of being the highest people lacking beneath in our condition.

I didn't discover any other mortals here in the present and its out-of-the-way line moment, unfamiliar circumferent. The torment lethality of Penac.

"Come here, we don't have time. All of you!" a strange man appeared with some peculiar words.

"Is there someone who knows him?" Marlen Balas shouted us.

"I can't tell yet." Brane Yares put out.

Everyone was mixed up with some unconnected thoughts baffled between the strange man and me.

"Come here! There's a Penac!" Another line he insisted.

"Exactly, we know there's a Penac but we didn't know you." Rion Hein mocked him.

Rion Hein talks for the first time, for us. He always got pencils in his belt I don't know why. A quiet person talked loud to be effective.

The strange man didn't answer. There's an intuition when we saw he's stepping back from us.

"What's your name?" Carrin Regra hesitated the man.

"I can't, I can't tell." The strange man stated.

"Why?" Yora Dence snapped.

"They are here! We have doomed" the strange man added, he run away.

"A lunatic." Katho Don countered and some of our members laugh off.

We knew Katho Don's ill-mannered, and some people like his rudeness.

I didn't find out it is funny. I knew Katho Don verbalize his view about what he just saw on that person. Nothing personal to him. People are sick for a long year since the Penac.

"I didn't know about Penac, even it's been a year since we got information in our temple, we are credulous." Marlen Balas grumbled to me.

"I think that too," I hissed while I'm rubbing my chest. Marlen Balas asks why I always do that. I muttered to him it's comfy.

{I don't want to tell them the truth about why I always rubbing my chest.}

"Tubby," Katho Don warned to me to put up some humor but nobody laughed. Yes, it's true. I'm a fat young man. Only Katho Don right now is blustery to insult me. I tolerably come about what happened, it's normal nothing is personal I go through that.

"Rubbing chest means he hungry." Katho Don cried. "Yeah," I pondered sarcastically.

There's no problem with him, only his tongue.

It's too early to be exhausted. In the Woil West Temple, we don't pray and worship for gods, we believe we are already connected to the creator of this world no matter what. Sometimes we meditate for our purpose when we don't know what to do, but more often we united for one goal and that goal is to help the outside people in the temple. Which currently change because of the spreading of Penac.

Along the road where we continued walking, we saw people in their balconies locking their Doors and windows.

For the first time we saw human acts but their acted weird, the question speculates why they do that belongs whether because of us or the Penac.

"Is this because of us?" Marlen Balas asked me a question that I'm not sure too, his tone of voice was like a child but he change when I recognized it. We have the same reasoning in some way.

The persuasion changed when we heard shattering sounds of the huge metallic-looking buzzer. We are all prepared for whatever happens except Katho Don, he got a sure-footed mental attitude.

****

Marlen Balas can't fight but I'm sure he can help me in the future, I don't know yet but I hope so. As we continued our walk the shady clouds that veiled the old houses disappeared and it's replaced by clear sunlight. We still had a view of the Woil West Temple as we walked down, still the same and unchanged except that we were farther away from the temple. It is not new to me that when someone sees me in the beam light I look up and close my eyes.

 I want to feel the non-toxic heat of the sun. It's been a long time since we got out of the Woil West Temple maybe it's okay that I didn't pass the trials, even though something harmful Penac was felt and we saw the outside of the temple again. Of the elders who have been my former temple Dotsets, they have been there longer, some of whom are from outside the Woil West Temple and others are children of officers but different from me. Our Honolio told me that a Nobleman had left me with him when I was little. It is not clear who and since there is nothing in the mouth of our Honolio to lie he confessed and told me the whole thing that happened in my life when I was a child. Continuing on the latter I still knew nothing continued of the Nobleman who had left me in the Woil West Temple. Maybe I can easily see them if there's a map here in this world. Maps need to be burned, as Penac gets worse every year.

Again we listened to our surroundings with the nine of my colleagues here, there was no certainty of the journey we were making so we only had one life chance and we had to take care of it.

We stop.

All of us frost, I saw the possible end of this journey quickly.

A headless man, a headless! This is the first time I saw a horrible death in my entire life.

"Penac, this is the Penac!" Katho Don warned. I saw his alarming anxious reaction to what was happening in front of us. Katho Don calming and cool behavior vanished when we saw a headless man. I can't handle the smell and what I'm looking for right now. In the end, I vomit.

"Wait! I recognized him! Th... That's Ercado's body! "Katho Don whispered and I can't believe he was him. "How do you know? " I reasoned Katho Don, I've got a doubt but in some case, if he was right it's very horrible welcome to us by the Penac.

"When we are in the temple I saw him wearing the bracelet just like that and he wearied an exact Krotolium (Woil West Temple Uniform) have you didn't notice that? Are you all blind?" Katho speculated and I imagined the body posture and his bracelet. I didn't compare to know if he is Vidia Ercado.

I didn't agree with what Katho Don replied but some of my colleagues agreed with him and Marlen Balas cried.

"Why are you crying?" Katho Don pondered Marlen.

"Really? You gonna ask me why I'm crying, idiot. Of course, he was one of us! I asked you, why you didn't even cry? Are you a psychopath? " Marlen Balas ventured Katho Don with a strong man tone that I didn't expect.

"That's normal, he deserves it." Katho Don exclaimed fast as he's trying to argue with Marlen Balas.

"What?" I hate when Katho Don insisted that. "Do you think his life is useless?"

"I didn't mean that you overacting. What's your problem?" Katho Don ask me as he didn't know why I'm getting mad.

"You! You are my problem."

"Me? Why?" Katho Don teased.

"You don't care about the life of Vidia Ercado. Someone died and you didn't feel anything, that's the problem." I added to him and lots of our colleagues looks at him.

"And... What's the problem with that?" He normally answered what I put forth without any facial reactions. " Do I need to pretend my emotion? Huhuhu Ercado why are you dead!" Katho Don sarcastically muttered to us.

Somebody laughed except me.

"Stop it! We need to go!" Marlen Balas passed on, as I believe and see he didn't laugh too.

"I don't want to argue right now, but please show some respect to the dead," I requested out loud to Katho Don and he annoyingly stared at me with a smile.

"Do you think, I'm a bad guy?" Katho Don added saying when we are walking.

"Stop it! All of you!" Marlen Balas warned at us.

We keep our mouths shut. We walk quietly but our blazing eyes of staring did not end.

The question of who killed Vidia Ercado was answered when we see in our way a huge man wearing a black fabric mask and holding a massive ax sharp-bladed with blood dropping in the grass.

"Run! All of you!" Marlen Balas stated to us. We don't know what our destination but we run separately. The man behind the black mask didn't chase us but he sway his massive bladed ax as he warned us to not disturb his territory.

The reason why I always get mad at my fellows is they are all annoying and unprepared, neither me.

****

I saw the very first assumption of the Penac.

Man bound to the spacious picture of the brutal

world is now I am. The sureness was eventually

falling apart to live happily in this place is false.

I saw chopped arms in the river's blood.

Dark pictures covered in blood color, I could not

understand because of the mud and worms

crawling on the very dirty ground that made me

vomit. One of the wrong directions went to me,

I heard screaming people afraid of death and

substitute cries of people who were murderers.

It was accompanied by the cries of the old man

and the grunts of the oppressed people.

My level of cowardice increased when I saw someone moving but without legs and crawling and saying "I'm gonna kill you." before I knew them I had strayed to where I should be, I remembered that I should follow whoever was holding the pendant given to us by our Honolio.

I know all of us ran. We ran in different ways I can't remember who the hell holds the pendant.

"Who holds the pendant!?" I shouted to a man running like me but he doesn't care about what I'm saying. I didn't know him at all but it seems he was one of us, a former Dotset I guessed.

Quietly dangerous around me I see people who are hungry and eager to kill their fellow man. Perhaps my lack of knowledge when it comes to Penac was too brutal and I did not expect this to be the case outside the temple.

I would rather die tired of running than have them stop my body parts.

It quickly left my mind as to whose Pendant our Honolio had given us.

I feel my foot ache but I don't even bother with it too much with someone chasing my murderers that I'm sure I already know their intentions towards me.

They have many spears, stones thrown at me. I was distracted but my chest was pounding so hard that all I could hear was my deep breathing that my Honolio taught me how to keep my breathing properly while diving far and action chase, those times I couldn't do it properly but now I understand that I need to pay attention to my breathing while I'm doing a fast and tiring run. I breathe deeply in such a way that I can breathe in enough air to give me a sustained breath in my run. I dodged those who were throwing stones at me when they hit me with a rock on my shoulder and I heard someone shout like a madman and he hit me successfully but it was not enough for me to stop running.

I lost sight of my comrades as I ran fast and

became chaotic. Our routes are for the lost and I

don't know where I should go.

Bang | Bump

Blind in the eyes of others, but the mind can clearly visualize them.

"Please open the door!" several times I tell people in their houses, I see them closing their doors as I run towards them. I feel that the weakness of my knees and feet as well as the rapid beating of my heart and the rise of acid from my stomach coincide with my feelings, my eyes also began to become blurred. I was able to hide from the pursuers for a while but I could still hear their voices. Searching in the little corner if there is opportunity that I could hide I still couldn't find anything. The first time I saw the beautiful light of the sky shine the heat of the sun touched my face. I lost my fear as I looked at the sky where the sunlight comes from I remembered the moments I was just a beginner in the temple, which I like the sunshine until now. In the sunshine I become calm. The peaceful chirping of my unidentified birds plays on my hearing. The colorful trees and ...

Suddenly the apprehension and fear returned to my mind when I heard again the madmen who wanted to kill me. I was able to hide in the little corner I'm sure they'll see me here when I'm not able to leave now. But when I suddenly ran I met The five or six murderer holding sharp spears and swords I again ran back from my passes and I kept asking for help from those who closed the door to their houses.

I hope there are still good people until now I need their help until I saw a house that opened their door, I saw them open the door for me and they wanted to let me in at first I was afraid it was just a trap but when I saw my man who looks like a carpenter who enters, he looks sober and trustworthy. I struggled to get out my fastest run just to reach the open door in the cement stone house as they chased me. I entered and immediately the carpenter-looking man closed his door and blocked it with a heavy cabinet. I need a few more minutes to get my natural breathing back I know I'm a bit fat and a lot of energy has been depleted in me and I'm non-stop running outside fortunately and someone opened the door and enters for me otherwise they can kill me tired and have no strength to resist.

"What are you doing outside kid?" Question of the man helping me.

"Yeah, believe it or not, I'm one of the people who live in the Woil West Temple," I explained to him as I chased him.

I tried to open my eyes. In the blocked cabinet of the carpenter-looking man I saw a man who was still hiding while my pursuers were shaking the closed door was bugling the cabinet door opened there I saw many heads and hands and a lot of blood came out, the first thought was correct I looked at the carpenter when I stared at him and immediately someone hit my head with a wooden stick that knocked me out of my consciousness.

****

My full name is Leodor Bumb, I am one of those who did not pass the exam and test of our Honolio I am from Woil West Temple along with The ten students who also did not pass we were allowed to prove ourselves in a mission to save people from Penac disease and also to save Our lives, using the Pendant given to us by our Honolio is just according to our Iowa guide to find the cure in Penac.

With annoyance mixed with regret, I lost sight of whoever The Penac holder was. One of the things I hated in my brain was that I forgot who holds the Pendant was when I just started running and after I ran so far that I almost fainted from what I went through, just live, I will fail and I will also get brutal people. I fainted, I can't remember what I saw while I was asleep I had a dream of a tomato floating and had weird useless dreams. When I woke up I first felt my hand ache which I knew was bound and harassed by brutal people with mental disease. It is inconceivable that they should kill and eat me now. I can't understand why I'm still alive and tied up.

"Lucky you kid, I got you." The man who let me into his house quaked that I knew he was a traitor and that I was fooled by his suit like a carpenter. All the brutal people shouted with mad up the hand of the man who helped me who also betrayed me himself, no he also seemed to be their leader.

I feel like it's a celebration I can't afford to see and I just want to close my eyes when I start to see punished people I don't know and while I accidentally see dead people and I suddenly get sick to smell.

I saw people with mental disease stare at me
when they saw my vomiting. I hope I also see
my friend Marlen Balas before they grill me like
a pig that I see in front of me as if they will cook
me worse than I expected that they should have
killed me than they would have cooked me
alive.

The strength of Marlen Balas is what I need here
or even the help of my mates but I failed to see
my comrades in this place I am surrounded by
murderers and fat, tall trees that I cannot see in
the morning or night.

It's natural for me to be scared and surprised by what I see now but now that I'm on the brink of death; I smile as if someone is telling me to laugh. I laughed, I didn't think about what would happen next as long as I was sure that they would kill me in seconds and minutes, my death was approaching.

People with mental disease marveled at me and they stopped laughing because they heard my laughter. I saw them in their faces and they thought I was mad and they looked at each other.

I do not know the name of the carpenter-looking man who helped and betrayed me but he ordered the sick people to lift the wood I was laying on to the fire they had lit in front of me.

I'm a heavy person and I weigh myself even more, until they fall on me which I intentionally do to make it harder for them to lift. I managed to drop me but I hurt myself when a large rock hit my mouth and hit me in the face when they dropped me.

The two sick mad men who were lifting me were bored and they tried to bite me on the hand and in my mouth with blood coming out due to the stone hitting my teeth.

It feels numb to the part of my mouth all I know

is there is bleeding and it is itchy. The carpenter-

looking man rebuked them and told to continue

carrying me to the fire where they would cook

me. I don't know how I would taste if they

stayed with me, for the rest of my life, only now

I can witness the person cooking and that's me.

I weighed myself down again I could only make

it harder for them to lift me. Maybe it's also my

advantage why I'm fat that I can slow down

their plan to cook me, I'm doing it for a long

time and I'm annoyed with those who lift me

that's my plan. As I see the carpenter-looking

man their leader smiles as his disciples lift me.

Maybe it's a miracle that I can survive them all I

can do is slow down my death. I expected to die

when the ones lifting me caught me and they suddenly dropped me again which I did not expect as if they meant to drop me and hit my mouth again and I felt the pain and soreness of my mouth even more.

Their screams of pleasure were replaced by screams of fear that I thought someone would save my life and I moved my head as I fell in front of the mud and tried to see who came but I failed to see it because I was in the wrong position. when I fall all I can see is the carpenter-looking man running and his disciples who are sick insane.

I felt blood on the side of my hand. In the first appearance, I assume that's human flesh and blood sprinkling out in my skin. When I heard a deep roaring beast that came out into my back I changed my thoughts that's not a human. A beast or a nightmare that would be my greatest problem in my ear a lot of thoughts came into what I heard analyzing them is not a good idea cause it's frightening me more than before, I prefer to be cook rather than a headless man. In some way I tried to remove the tight straps on my hand I was trying to get away because this was my chance to escape if I was lucky, but suddenly someone pulled on my back that looked like a giant and strong to lift me like a dog, I know that was the monster I could hear and I felt the sharpness of his tooth and the breath of his mouth in my head as if he intended to eat me alive.

***

Shouting out loud doesn't change the event why would I even do that if I already knew the next events would happen to me. It was painful and forced to bury and I felt that the demon was destroying my skull with the help of blood as if I had been given a crown of thorns to be crushed by the padding wrapped around my head. I wanted to shout but I didn't. It would be better for me to die quietly than for him to know I am afraid of death.

I regained all my courage and indifference to my life when I heard the cry of a man who was afraid to die and I also cried for my life. When I shouted for help from a stranger I did not know and he suddenly threw stones at the dangerous creature that would have killed me, my vision was a bit blurred and my surroundings were covered with growing ancient trees, a shadow added to my fear turning into a nightmare.

I lost the bondage to the wood as the dangerous creature broke it, lost, and removed the thick rope that had tormented me before. I ran a bit to escape and got stuck in the place of the insane people with mental disease. Suddenly my eyes ached with my blood dripping from my head. Again, I heard the creature that was going to kill me. I immediately turned around to see who that dangerous creature was and saw he was also the one we had all seen before, the big creature holding the big spear before we all parted apart I ran to black and smoky colors wherever you can run and hide. It's no joke that this creature is the size of my body with one hand so he immediately grabbed me like a dog earlier. The one who was fighting against him who I thought was my ally was not a real ally, the carpenter -looking and his staff with the sick mad rebelled against the monster that I heard the carpenter-looking man order his disciples to kill me. I was alarmed by this because two sides wanted to kill and eat me. A large and dangerous creature and starving dead with insane disease. This event was very brutal because as I was running I could see the giant creature throwing at me his enemy who wanted to kill and expel me like an ant.

I followed the smoke part of the forest, chance it was dark and I could not be seen immediately, I hid like a frightened rat. The cruelty of the opportunity deliberately landed in my palms.

I ran fast even though I couldn't see my path and I'm sure my pursuers couldn't see it either because I could hear their annoyance as I was running straight into this area. I stumbled to see the end of my run but I thought of hiding and rolled to the darkest part where I could hide.

I was able to hide well, holding my breath moving so that they could not see me under the muddy and dark place where I was lying.

This certainty is certain if they can't track me

down here under the muddy, even if I can hear

their footsteps and voices around me I am

limited to making any noise. This situation

lasted only seconds.

I thought I could survive the danger but here I

was wrong. The mud I thought I was holding

and where I was lying was not mud but bloody

spattered. I didn't notice it right away and it

took full attention to see the sticky and viscous

look of mud but blood.

I don't think they are blood but my brain tries to

remind me that I am lying on my back and in the

blood, the smells are stamping on me that my

stomach can't tolerate what I see and smell, I

keep from vomiting I want to get rid of I can

sense the smell but I can't. I wanted to cover my

nose but I couldn't do it either because my two

hands were soaked in the blood mud where I

was lying.

My pursuers had left, I could no longer hear

noises like the ones I had heard before.

Only the sound of insects and the melody of the

wind beating on the trees, plants, and grass are

all I can hear now until I heard the growl of a madman laughing which alarmed me when suddenly someone pulled my legs and stabbed me I don't know what but small prickly wood leaving marks and small spikes leftover wood on my side. I tried to get away but it was too late he tried to stab me with a wooden knife in the side of my nape. It was insane and painful but I started to close my eyes and couldn't fight because my muscles were weakening and I couldn't move my whole body. I was annoyed because I had never seen an enemy before and they always attacked me from behind as if I was an animal they were chasing and I always had nothing against them.

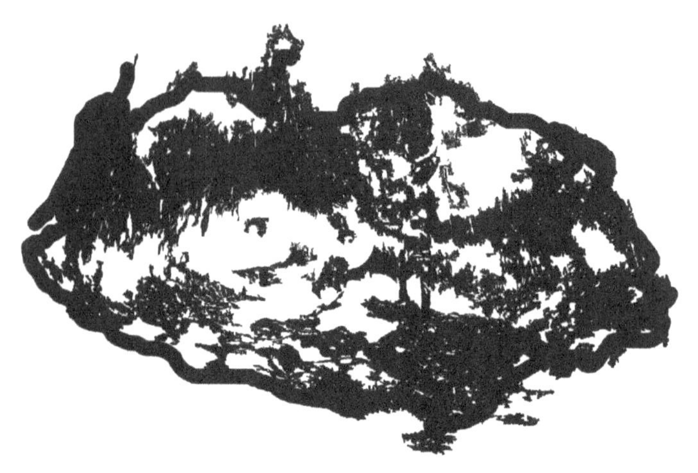

Grot·to

Walk straight and still get lost.

I knew my whole body had collapsed, even before I opened my eyes I was sure I was lying on a soft bed. The piercings on my side and the irritating side of my neck are now a barrier to my comfort. I heard the sharpening and walking sound and movement of a man on my right side. I have not yet opened my eyes and my only use is my senses and my ears. I let my whole body rest while my mind worked. I was drowned in death and buried my feet in the ground full of a mixture of mud and blood. Making sure my knees and feet were moving and complete before I acted on my next plan.

***

I didn't expect the sudden itching of my throat I couldn't stop and suddenly my mouth made a noise, I coughed.

 I backed away suddenly, I slapped myself in disbelief. I heard the madman holding a wooden knife, the looks of the lion creature overflowing with anger the small voice of irritation I heard in his mouth.

***

As I stood up while observing his actions I felt weakness in my head and I suddenly felt something I should not care about ...

"I'm hungry" I meant to tell him because I couldn't stand it anymore. My brain decided that whatever food I would eat, just to lose my hunger.

The mad man holding the wooden knife didn't speak, but instead,he just let me stand and walk while I tried to move slowly. I had no language to understand him as if I were talking to a caveman.

"How long have you been here?" I asked him hoping he understood me but he didn't say anything and he just ignored what I sobbed.

"Are you a monkey man?" I even asked him to make sure he didn't understand me before I made another plan to leave his territory.

 He approached me, I suddenly backed away. I didn't know what he would do to me after I insulted him he suddenly raised his legs as if he was making me smell it. I thought he was going to kick me but I was wrong. I also proved that he was not among the sick madness people because he did not have any temptation to eat me alive. I'm lucky, and here I am and I don't want to feed my whole body to the insane people who are sick of eating me. But I didn't know his language and what he planned for me.

I tried to go to the table and he just let me walk again I saw containers of wines and fruit that were green and shaped like the shape of a human face fruit. As I look at his food and water on the table I also observe the human monkey. I know my life is dangerous to him I can only make a bad mistake that I do not know that he can crawl and maybe he will suddenly stab me with I'm not ready. I saw that he didn't care when I picked a fruit that I didn't know what to call it because I was also sure if it was food, so I thought of throwing it at him and seeing how he would react. I threw the fruit on his table at the monkey man and he looked at me badly, as he took the fruit with his right hand he didn't lose his bad look at me as he did this I looked at what he do to the one I threw a fruit. He immediately

grabbed it and was about to throw it at me hard

and I suddenly blocked my hand just to avoid it.

I guessed wrong.

He suddenly bit it and chewed it, I nodded at

him and I joaked the word "Food" to him, he

didn't understand me and he turned to me as if

he didn't want to talk to me and I just let him do

what he wanted to do.

 I saw two more fruits like the one I threw at him

and as he did, I tried to bite and chew them.

 I regretted it because what I tasted like shit I thought about how he ate it met and raised my eyebrow, I immediately turned around again to him and saw him turn around and chew. I can say it's safe to eat the food I tried to spit out my first bite of fruit but when I saw him again biting and chewing while turning around I also tried what he was doing but now after I chewed quickly I immediately swallowed it, no longer think about the taste and whatever this food is called, I will eat it. I need energy, even if my stomach can't stand it I still try to consume it. This is the only thing I know to survive in this cave and to the outside.

If sick people with Penac attack here in the cave, what will we do? And if the human-ape kills me in this cave what else can I use against it? Questions spontaneously enter my mind. While eating I saw an opportunity to look for a wooden knife on the table, I didn't immediately pick it up although I made sure the male monkey still turned his back. The opportunity was dictated by at the right time, I quickly took the wooden knife, and when I touched it ...

 I made a mistake and I underestimated the ape-man too much. I quickly let go of the wooden knife, I didn't continue my plan, his full force was ready when I felt his breath in the back and there was a sharp knife in my neck that I was sure he would kill me if I continued to pick up the sharp wood on his table.

"It's fine, I'm not going to do it," I went on to him. I surrendered. He didn't remove yet the knife pointing to my neck, there was a language barrier between us, so I acted as I begging for my life hopefully he can understand what I'm trying to do.

I step little by little away from the table and to the knife and he stayed in the position near the table. He looked seriously sharp of his eyes are similar to an aggressive beast. I sat on the ground hopefully he would stop staring at me.

***

I avoided opportunities to fight. I don't want to add those who will kill me. I hope that at the moment, I am here we will also get along with this ape-man. I signaled to him that what I knew would help me lower his suspicions that I would attack him.

I thought of stopping and sitting slowly near the kindled fire he had made that served as a light in this cave. I had no plans to put out the fire because I didn't familiar with the cave which compared to him he was veteran a firewood shovel in the fire and the wood was already in the fire itself so I immediately raised my two hands and showed it to the monkey man who was with me, I raised my two hands signaling that message I will not resist. I immediately stepped back to the side and stood next to the fire and there and sat down. As I watched him he was still looking at me and his eyes were still wrapped in doubt but I turned my gaze away from him and out of the corner of my eyes, I knew he was continuing to eat the fruit I had thrown at him earlier.

Not far away I heard a bad sound that would bring us misfortune. I heard the scream of the man, I suspected were people sicked in Penac. In this situation the caveman next to me became aggressive and he left his stand. I left the problem to him that I knew he knew what he was going to do because since he had been in this area for so long he had memorized all the edges as well as the exact location of what we had heard.

After he left I did what I should have done earlier to pick up the wooden knife on the table, I immediately hurried and opened my two eyes in anticipation of getting the wooden knife, but I could not see it I immediately cut the fruit and other items on the table but no longer the wooden knife. There I began to lose interest in the ability to think of a caveman and here I found out that he still did not trust me fully matched because with this ability I also did not criticize him properly, the stabbing he did stick in my mind on my back and I didn't fight with that sleeping attack and strategies.

***

I couldn't bear to fight, my mind was shrouded in darkness even revenge or avoiding the sick Penac was too deep in my view. I want to kill an opponent. As I sat I heard a dog barking. This is unusual because since before and in the past, I have walked outside the temple I haven't seen any dead or living animals, I seem to have caught the attention of people with Penac disease and lost my mind that there are still animals in this place. As the voices of those, I had heard from before faded away it became mysterious that I was just obsessed to look in which direction I heard the dog barking that I think I was just so close to it here in the cave.

As I walked the surroundings gradually became so quiet that I no longer knew how I would see the dog barking before. The direction I was going was right but I hadn't finished knowing it when I suddenly lost my direction without the dog noise. The place where I was facing was a bit dark and my horizon was only backward because of the light made by the caveman.

I heard the dog barking again, but this time the sound of its barking was far away from me so instead of chasing the sound I just went back to my source. As I walked back I was greeted by two bloody people standing with their eyes closed. They suddenly fell and I was shocked that they were dead and the caveman was just lifting them.

 "What are those?" I asked him as he let go and kicked the sick Penacs he had killed.

The first time he answered me and I heard a vocal voice that suited humane conversation. He told me the word "Penac" and I nodded at him and I didn't respond a word. This time he decided to sit down and continue his meal while I imitated what he did. We waited a few minutes to take the time, I slowly moved the wood I had watered earlier that was on the fire to keep our light on while he was silent, scratching his arm and staring at the fire. I, on the other hand, decided to close my eyes for a moment and thought that nothing bad would happen to me, I knew that the caveman wouldn't kill me. The brave hands and fingers he was buried in the ground was treading, were gone as well as the annoyance and anger in his mouth and eyes, I could no longer see. The

caveman became so calm that I would no longer

obstruct his thinking because of the little

hardships. I was doing not to do bad that I think

I had left the undesirable activities in his eyes.

Fortunately, I was able to do it too eventually.

Silence is in my hands and I can sleep peacefully

without fear. The caveman creature that I am

with is a reliable friend and I don't want him to

think differently of me as an enemy right now if

I predict the events now I am inside the cave

with a dangerous caveman and I agree that by

myself. While taking a nap I immediately heard

the repeated sound of water as if there was rain

around us, I looked where the rain was coming

from, I noticed the caveman did not take his eyes off the fire even though I was standing. I heard the dog barking again but now the sound of the dog barking is crying which worries me because the dog I heard now seems to be asking for help and it is different before compared.

I was hesitant to do anything but I couldn't stand a crying animal especially a dog so I decided to go ahead and watch the crying dog barking what was happening.But before I did that I looked into the caveman's eyes again who looks straight ahead and full attention to the fire that is lit.

I went back to the walk, I had stopped earlier here in the cave. Now, as I'm stepping in the direction here in the cave where I can hear the dog barking I'm going away in the light of the fire, it's a bit scary but I don't think too much about the negative that will come out or happen to me. My mission to save the dog is in my to-dos.

My knees were shaking, but I was still walking. I remained a brave coward.

Straight walk mixed with nervousness,

fortunately, I can also hear the straight barking

of the dog. I accelerated my walk a little,

because also in the loud voice that I repeatedly

heard outside or in whatever was wrapped in

this cave I could hear the rain.

The noise of the surroundings flowed through

my body and nature called me suddenly, I want

to pee.

I stopped walking and stood on the side of the

cave, I was walking in and there I followed the

flowing water that sounded like rain. After I did

that I resumed my interrupted mission but I was

a little confused and lost my concentration when

I touched the side of the cave and I had a small

hole that touched the cave a bit rough and can be

scratched on the skin the cave looks like a wall, I

thought peek I dug a hole in the cave but I

couldn't see anything but when I put my ear to it

I knew that the rain was coming from outside.

Trog·lo·dyte

Real warriors will win the war, even they are defeated.

When I heard the rain coming from outside the cave I thought of wading in the middle of the darkness, I was treading on. I didn't continue the search for the dog. I lay down because this is what I used to do in the temple when it rains, I fall asleep. I want to sleep while it's raining because this is what my body is looking for and I feel calm mentally as I listen to the rain while lying down and I fall asleep voluntarily.

 Unbeknownst to me, I also felt pain in my right ear as if there was a recurring pain that I could not identify, including in my right eye but for a few seconds, they also disappeared.

Maybe it's because of the fatigue that I experienced and the battles that I ran to survive, my eyes also began to blur, which I felt at first because my surroundings were dark here on the path where I lay quite well and rough but tolerable.

I don't feel any pain but I'm weak and tired from the indefinite feeling that maybe I haven't slept enough before and I still need to regain the strength to sleep to continue. I fell asleep until I felt a tickling tongue on my right cheek I quickly opened my eyes and there I noticed the dog I was looking for.

I smiled with joy and lost my sleep that the dog

found me and I did not have to continue

walking here in the dark part of the cave, I tried

to lift the dog and I noticed that he had a wound

on his back and could I think his wound is

hardening and it's pretty hard as if he's scared.

This dog suffered.

I swear whoever does this I will kill. I don't kill

but when I see someone hurting a dog and any

animal life is a substitute. I can't bear myself to

get angry when I see a coveted dog. I

can't stand people committing brutality to animals. Even though I was in the Woil West Temple, I cared more about the welfare of the animals than the people in the temple. I immediately stood up and obliged myself to assume responsibility for caring for the dog that I saw. His face was gentle, he was watching my reaction and I looked at him the same way as he looked at me. He was a bit heavy, but I was able to carry him to my place with my caveman. As I walked towards my treadmill my feet were a bit obsessed with what I was treading lost in my mind was that we didn't have slippers or any other foot protection. My clothes are also dirty and unrepresentable, covered in mud and blood clots, because of my running, hiding, and rolling on the ground and dead people can only survive the disaster.

If I relate how I feel, I know better the emotion of the dog I am caring up.

***

I was tamed by the soft voice of the dog. Based on his actions the dog wanted the tenderness of him licking my left arm as I lifted him towards the light fire made by the caveman.

As I walked there, my left foot suddenly itched like an insect was biting, I tried to put up with it, because we were close to the firelight but as I pushed and continued to walk it itched even

more that I had to stop for a while. The dog
could still wait. I immediately let go of the dog
for a moment scratched my left foot and looked
for where and what insect was biting me. I was
disappointed to see the insect, I just scratched
my foot as the itching changed. I would rather
have my wound hurt than an itch. I continued
to scratch while the dog hurried to the beam of
fire where we were staying the caveman, I let the
dog, I was confident that he could get to where
we should go. I scratched the itchy foot until it
was a bit sore it was okay than before.

 I continued to walk towards the light fire I
could see, where I was hanging and as I got
closer I could see fresh blood, I was worried

about the drops of blood I saw, I knew these

wounds were from the dog.

 My feet spontaneously hurried and I proved to

myself that I could run straight fast and even

though I didn't memorize the dark ground, I

was treading and ignored it just to get to where I

was going. I felt the painful and small stones

that I stepped on. But I did not bear it,

sometimes it hurts, but I don't stop walking just

to get to the path of the dog I would have

helped. I got to the firelight where I had come

from earlier.

The wound and pain of my senses were deep in my feet and there were small stones buried that pierced because of the weight of my body as I walked, so did the stones that stuck to my feet. I immediately removed the small stones that were piercing my feet while looking at where the dog, I was going to help.

I was shocked and suddenly the size opened my eyes. I was carried away by my emotions. Suddenly there were tears in my eyes.

The dog's nerves deepened and now he is unconscious. My dog is dead, I wish I could help.

I saw the caveman his sharp nails in his hands were proof that he was the culprit in the dog's death. My eyes darkened and I suddenly lost control of my actions, I wanted to kill the caveman, I wanted to attack him and pluck his eyes and strip, cut off his body part as he did in the dog, however!

But!

However.

I can't do it.

***

My hands and jaw tremble in anger I feel angry as my will throbs at the event I see in the dog's condition. I can't quite imagine them happening.

While I can see that killing a dog that has no opponent is nothing in the cave, I want to take revenge on the animal he killed. But someone stopped me from attacking the caveman because I was afraid of losing an ally when I was in danger and it was obvious that he was an expert in fighting and being resilient compared to me but his intellect and compassion were probably lost in his brain is what I have and we can work together but I have to let go of my anger first because if I can't control it might just cause a bad fight between me and my fellow caveman. Suddenly the height of my skull hurt as if I had a headache that I didn't know why maybe I was holding back my anger and annoyance at what the caveman did to the dog.

"Why," I asked him but I did not put my words in a questioning tone.

I strained to be calm, waiting for the right opportunity to vent the anger I couldn't. I can't change the expression of anger on my forehead that my two eyebrows meet spontaneously as if whatever I do to make my face look calm, I can't do that even my looks I know are getting irritable. I could feel my left earache at the noise I heard in the part where I came from and what I saw in the dark part of the cave.

The caveman tried to look at me and I immediately turned around so he couldn't see the angry face I had that I couldn't control with the dog he killed. The saying that sleep is needed to be strong is that the first thing I did was lie down on the path instead of finding out what I heard in the dark part of the cave again I thought not to go and I just lay down near the fire while the caveman did. I could hear the roaring tiger sound angrily as if someone was trying to frighten me. I couldn't see what he was doing because I was lying down and positioned in the back where he couldn't see the expression on my face. After all, until now I couldn't accept what he did to the dog with no opponent against.

     "Penac! Penac!" words came out of his mouth and suddenly my drowsiness was interrupted, here I witnessed him say Penac twice as if he was signaling or implying to me that I needed to be prepared for the event that would happen here. I immediately stood up to see and witness where the caveman was looking. He was looking in the other direction where I was standing the direction, he was looking was the piercing mold of large chunks of rocks that seemed dangerous to go for tall people. Maybe the caveman also knows that he can't go to it, because he is worried about the size of his body and his height is not suitable for him to go.

In our preoccupation, I decided to take whatever stick I could if any enemy was coming the caveman saw me looking but he didn't pay attention to me and focused his attention sin, where I suspected the enemy came out and went. I didn't see anything I could whip or stick that could be slapped but I got a chance to pick up the small rocks that pierced my foot before, this is the only way I know to, at least help the caveman and we can't get in of the opponent or anyone with Penac disease. I stood on the side chance that I could not immediately see anyone coming out of the small hole of the cave that was shrouded in darkness. As the caveman stood in the middle to greet the opponent, he showed and heard a voice that seemed to have a mixture of tiger sound and anger towards our future opponent. I hope that whoever comes out of the small hole of the cave will be frightened.

 As we waited for her to come out I could already hear her steps and the soothing sound as we waited was the intensification of the steps we were hearing.

We knew that whoever was going to show up here in the small hole of the cave was about to arrive but we were surprised that he suddenly fell silent, and lost the loud sounds of his steps as if he had observed us waiting to attack him. The caveman thought of turning off the light he had made on the fire.

Now we both have nothing to see and the person who comes out I also can't see, only the dark reflection that is dirty blue I don't know where our light comes from that in the extreme darkness I can't move, because I'm afraid that with a formidable enemy or worse. I'm worried that I'll hit the caveman and he'll attack me instead of the enemy. I could hear the caveman's deep breathing but it was also quiet and he had removed the threatening voice he had been making before. I knew that on the left side of my ear was the position where I was listening to the noises from the small hole in the cave that we suspected would come out and the caveman was on the right side where my attention was focused on listening to the caveman who turned off the light. I immediately folded and bowed

because in the darkness I could see it was even

more dangerous for me to be hit and mistaken

for a caveman who was an enemy and I was

afraid he would kill me unintentionally like the

dog I would have protected.

 I remember our Honolio. He taught us the

importance of when we will not fight and when

we will fight I believe I carry the principle and

that principle is being a good leader that even if I

am not a leader at least I know how to give up

especially when the goodness and welfare of my

member's life and my own life would be in

danger in my way.

I heard a crisp sound that I immediately paid attention to avoid whatever I heard if it was an attack as long as I was able to avoid it otherwise it would have been okay, I immediately squeezed myself to the very edge of the cave that was in I am also safe. I didn't show I was a coward because first of all they didn't see me hiding like a coward and second of all the caveman wouldn't laugh at me. After all, he didn't know the word and deed of cowardice. My situation began to change and I felt when I heard the loud and angry shout of the caveman as if he was hurt by the not-so-distant voice that I heard, I could not identify because also the echo emitted and dictated by the cave was blind. I'm like a bat that I have to bump myself into things I want to know the situation, I'm not doing and I know I'm going to ruin the stand and all I can do is squeeze myself to the side. As I lay on the edge of the chaos I could feel the coldness of the rock I was holding and large chunks that were on the edge of the cave, very cold and refreshing and I wanted to stick my whole body to it for my safety and fixation. feeling until I sneezed inadvertently I tried to suppress and pass in silence sneezing but I did not immediately cover it with my hands right away. I know the caveman and his enemies heard this suddenly fell silent for a moment and the caveman made a noise that I think he thinks of me as an enemy that as I thought before is gradually matching these chaotic events. I can't hear the noise of the caveman's opponent but I know that the caveman's anger is focused on me when he hears me sneezing in the darkness and the illusion that he made himself that I can be ruined and taken back to life so before he does. and before he could hit me with any deadly attack my crawling and rolling became action and just got away from the voice of the caveman and his enemy, I was quietly rolling and crawling away from my position I knew, I would be hit by whoever could track me down so I decided to crawl quietly away from the problem.

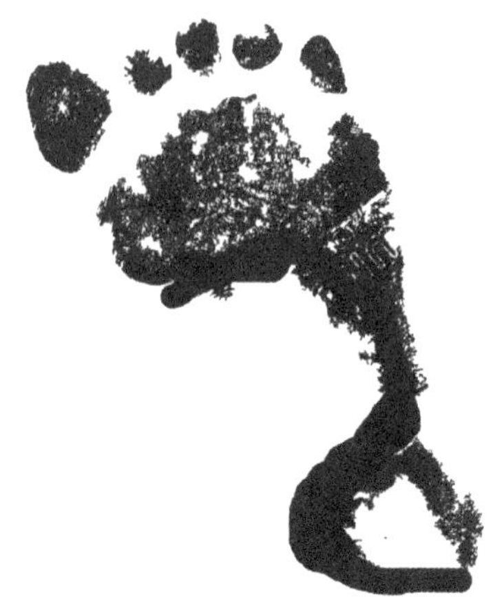

/märk/

Some can see hope in the eyes of a child, but the process of hope depends on us.

As I crawled, I found a small foot, a

child's foot. I'm sure it was the child's

foot. I can't say this to the caveman

because until now he is still lost and the

dirt and dust. I can touch in the cave

clings to my finger which seems to itch

my skin.

I try not to let the dirt hit the wounds I

have received, which I am worried about

getting infected due to dizziness and

headaches. Sleepy but I have to keep

going.

I heard the child's footsteps in a direction I didn't know where to go. My eyes hurt when I try to open, clear and force my eyes to look at the things I see in the darkness, I don't understand why the caveman turned off the light source which I certainly wouldn't be harmed if whoever came in earlier, now we have a hard time being clear everything that is happening around us when I fall. I know when I stand up it is more dangerous, I am afraid of being hit or punched by a caveman. I continue to crawl again to where I heard the footsteps of the boy I didn't know who and how he was able to get past it quickly in the very dark surroundings.

The man of fear falls deep into the push to develop into becoming a hard spiky stone. I felt the courage but safety is a good act. The cave is big in the dark. I'm blind to estimating my speed and moving when I crawl. The only voice I heard was the caveman, not the kid.

In the thickness of the dust, I was rolling I could feel the dust. I was inhaling was quite fine and suddenly it stuck to my nose, I slightly raised my head to avoid a bit of the dust I was inhaling. As I retreated, I suddenly heard a loud crash behind me as if someone was throwing a large chunk of rock that I immediately avoided and returned to my crawl and continued quickly, avoiding breathing continuously and preventing me from being hit by the chunk of rock where I am being followed.

I feel the rocks approaching because it

sticks to the king's arms and thighs which

when I don't move I know I will lose

consciousness with the force of throwing

the rock whoever is throwing, I have a

big doubt that the caveman is so angry

because he can't see his opponent either.

In my haste to crawl, I ignored the ones

that fell into my pocket, which I thought I

couldn't use anymore.

I knew that the pebbles I had collected were gradually falling into my pocket earlier so that in case the enemy entered the cave he would receive many irritating and stinging stones. My scars and scratches on my foot I also know are already covered with dust and soil from the side of the cave where I crawl quickly just stuck to the caveman that when while I was listening I knew I was still in danger of being hit. Again, I wondered at the kid running straight in the direction I believe this is also where he ran. I try to find his movements with my ear and his footsteps but as I continue this my ear is confused because the caveman is missing.

With the tiring crawl I knew, I was about to succeed. Little by little the noises I could hear in the caveman were fading. But I was still lost because I didn't know where the child, I had been following had gone. I immediately turned my attention to my nose as it was already itching because of the dust I had inhaled.

They're not good for my health, I am sure

I will die if I continue to crawl so I

thought of getting up and eating my

footsteps and things,I avoid colliding

with.

 I continued to walk even though I was

blind in the darkness, I gradually heard

the hope I wanted to see. I heard that

there seemed to be a fire burning right in

front of me where I was walking a little if

I am not mistaken, there was another

person or caveman in this area and not just that aggressive caveman, I had seen before. The success that I got away from the caveman who was eager to fight, I hope I am faithful to the good and calm man or the caveman now. I stopped walking when I saw someone making a wood-burning fire, I didn't want to startle someone and stop what he was doing because when he heard my actions he would not be able to light the fire he was lighting.

I waited as long as I could. Even though I could not step without him, seeing or hearing I was desperate for the light.

At Woil West Temple I have always been unable to make good decisions whenever necessary, when choosing the right and proper decision. I know right and wrong but when I come out of that place and I'm stuck here now I'm not sure if I'm going to do good deeds or I need to do better.

At the Woil West Temple, the first

commandment of all our Honolio is that

we are not allowed to kill anything alive.

My first sin was that I killed all kinds of

insects every night. I couldn't avoid it. I

didn't notice it and told my fellow

students in the temple that I was killing

insects. I didn't tell them stories. besides

a friend of mine.

 The fire I was waiting for was about to be

lit, in seconds and minutes I would see

that whoever was making the fire, I

hoped it was just a child lighting it

because I knew that what I was following

was in the same direction. I waited and

kept my eyes on the person, I was looking

forward to.

 No fun and noise I made as I saw that he

had successfully turned on the light the

fact was happy and I was already

screaming with joy and it could be seen in

my fingers and joy in the eyes. But ...

 however.

He suddenly blow it when he heard the barking of a dog. I lost my mind and turned my attention to which dog was barking. The face of the dog I helped that was killed by the caveman touched my breath. But it's impossible, it's so wrong to think that dog is still alive that I know it's time the dog isn't moving and breathing.

Limited evidence and misleading hopes.

The insertion of the crisp sound of a leaf in my ear signaled that the man who had put out his fire was walking in the darkness. I couldn't tell him that I wasn't dangerous because the wood I was carrying was ready in case I was really against him.

Closing my eyes, I waited for the opportunity to walk into the smoke of the fire he had lit and extinguished.

There I focused my senses while embracing the belief that good creatures are not as aggressive as the caveman I first saw.

Slow steps, along with the ready stick in case there's something I didn't expect. I tried to figure out where I was walking with my left hand in conjunction with my right foot making sure my next steps wouldn't be dangerous.

The pinky branch of the tree sank deep into my feet it hurts. He resembled a plant I didn't expect to have in the cave, I would hardly see in the very dark corner I was standing on, and if I were to describe it based on how I felt it was as if I had touched a cactus that seemed to hurt so much when I pushed my right toes on my foot. I felt the pain but I didn't stop and I remained ready I didn't think to respond but my defensive tactics changed and I slowly acted more and more as I tried to approach the smoke I smelled being blown by someone who didn't confirm what he looks like.

My motivation is scattered by a lazy behavior strike in my blood. Slowly divided weakness feeling in my left to right feet, no anxious feelings.
The encounter part of describing the lost strength replace by the calmness of mind.
A meditation of focusing my breath and hearing the inner circulation of my brain or the frequency level of the cave remained unto my ears.

In my above, for the first time, I saw the rock formation of the flowstone. The flashy whiteness remained a mystery as I observed in the blink of the eye I knew and I can observe my surroundings in a second before the toxic sleep ran out to eliminate my consciousness. It's a trap that I felt when I collapsed early same feeling when the caveman chop me with a thorn of a crimson knife in my first encounter with him, but this time it's much less hurt compared to the knife. The webs, the dust, and the last thing I touched is the rock that slid downward faster in a side of the cave, first I felt. It seems like a trap but as long as the time passed each second I discovered smooth downward, my world changed with no pressure or hurt in my bruises like I took a Valerian root herb to make me feel sleep little and faster as I didn't expect.

Fast beating and destructive tiring running, I suffer breathlessly and every discomfort of my footsteps is several with liquid that when it looks like blood.

I couldn't see the drastic I was getting on to me and I wasn't sure in my mentality why I was commending it. Moving quickly and dehydrating sniffing for breath clogs my chest. Every minute I perceive a concern that I don't know strictly where it's reaching from. It was so problematic and I unawares began to scream because I didn't remember the reason for the looming threats that my brain was performing while I was fleeing, I was continuously doubtful that no matter who was hustling me, I would not heed a voice or a shade of the opponent.

I needed to stop sprinting so fast and catch my breath that I felt it wasn't over yet and I could do triviality but run as rapidly as I could. I keep in mind that it's okay and avoid this turmoil that I resist informing myself over and over again.

***

I woke up experiencing heavy. It was all just a nightmare. The feeling that I was in difficulty went on, with as I eventually woke up. My heart was still beating fast and I couldn't calm myself down from what was coming about even though nothing was happening. I immediately looked at the fire, went back to my recollection of the little things that had occurred and I tried to remember the other events until I finally understood the additional answers to my questions in my intellectual when I saw the caveman perking up and serious, his eyes stared directly into my visions he was confused but he knew I was terrified he backed away a bit because his huge expression first appeared to me which would give me heart illness if he hadn't backed down I would faint. I motioned him with my hands not to come near me and he obeyed me for the first time. After that I felt my chest still throbbing, feeling that I was in danger, I calmed myself that I knew I wasn't this worst before. It's not easy for me to get scared when I know I'm in danger the more I used to. But now worryingly, this world has already changed me.

"How did you get here?" Voice of the child I don't know where. I didn't answer it but tried to rule out my eyes from whom the voice that suddenly spoke came from. My attention was somewhat diverted to the present event after I heard the child's voice. I heard the vibrations and footsteps that sounded like the noise of wood that accompanied the beating I heard my heartbeat because of fear earlier. Being confined in a cave is very strange because I can hear the echoes and the noise of my body as well

as in my courtyard every time I close my
eyes I hear the sound as if I am in another
dimension.

 Next, a small creature appeared behind
the caveman. To this day I still can't
believe that the dog I thought was dead is
alive and can walk quite well. I was
wrong in judging the caveman. I proved
he wasn't that brutal to the animal and
here I realized that he had cured the dog
with the stinging and sleepy thing I
thought was poison.

I immediately touched my foot to caress my wounds and it was gone. They cured me I don't know how many days and I don't know if morning and night are out.

 "Who let you into our territory?" Next question of the small voice I heard that if listened to carefully I was sure only a child was speaking.
I still didn't answer until I heard the wooden footsteps again which I determined in which direction I could

hear them and it was there behind the big

man cave. Suddenly the little head

peeked that my prediction was correct

and I was a little surprised because he

doesn't have legs with only wooden legs

he uses to walk which until now I still

can't believe how he balances his body

with two sticks which serve as his thigh

and foot in walking.

"The man in the cafe next to you let me in

here.

I want to get out of this place and I have to join my group to eradicate Penac disease. Can you help me get out of this place? How can you do that? Are people with Penac disease prevented from entering here? "I asked the boy walking with the two sticks he was using for walking. He walks so fast that I can compare him to a real foot.

 "It's too early to leave this area. Opponents are surrounding the cave we're standing in, believe it or not, we can stop people with Penac disease using our sleeping knives." He told me quite seriously that it was like I was just his age, how he talked and I was innovating in some way but strange because his voice didn't match how he delivered.

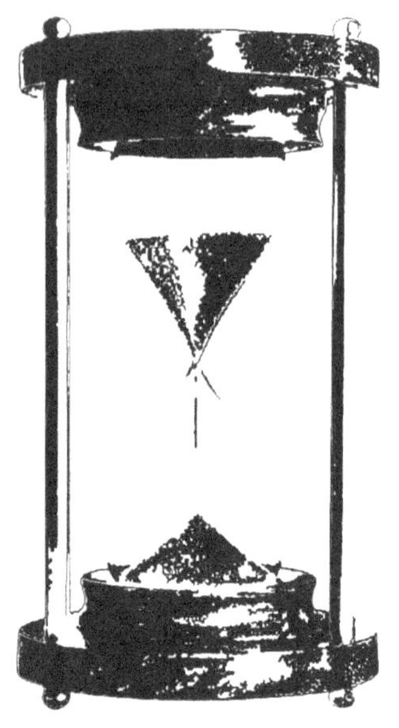

/ˈtīmˌpēs/

We don't have enough time here in this world to find true peace other than beliefs.

If you think from the opposite perspective I know I am doing the right thing interacting with them.

 I added the opposite because I knew it wouldn't work but I still tried to see the possibility. I wanted to agree with my own this time so that they could help me get out, what I ventured was purely away from the cave area we were standing.

 I remember that I had an important mission to fulfill and that was to save others from this disease that I knew if I just stayed nothing would happen to the three of us here and I would just wake up to the fear outside so maybe this is the right time for taking a step. I am referring to leave the cave I can't see and the possibility is closed due to the darkness of the surroundings and I believe there is a wide barrier of obstacles that lurked in every stone cave this century ago.

My desire to get out of here is overflowing.

"Will you help me?" I asked them.

"Why?" A child asked me again if I could speak as if I was talking to someone as old as me.

Maybe I'm just used to the fact that when the child talks to me I can see in his posture and speech the humility because in our temple I learned their manners are both I'm a bit insulted in the young cave that is here but I just let it go because there is nothing I can do if I stand up to criticize his behavior.

 Sweating part of my thigh I knew the ticklish little drop of sweat was flowing down my foot as I waited and wondered what a good answer to his question why.

 "Our Honolio has given us a mission." I don't know if this kid knows what Honolio means.

Because I knew in myself that he couldn't know something like that, which size from the place I came from it was so far from this cave area. The strength and training I did in my study of the area were based on the number of steps I counted when I left my temple home. I'm over five thousand steps walk and run so I'm making sure he can't pinpoint and know what the word Honolio means.

 "Honolio ?!" Word of the child I am not sure if his questioning or hostile backward response he tells me. I thought of returning the word I responded to him and back he asked me and I changed my tone to make sure the word I was implying was "Honolio."

"What Honolio?" The child expressed and here I proved that destiny agrees with me as he does not know these words I am sure the plan agrees with me.

"This is a man who occupies the world and I will work with him now that if I do not leave this place he will destroy the whole cave, I am here to serve as a warning, and when you kill me thousands of soldiers will come to destroy the thick this cave.

However, if you release and help me to get out of this place I will not make a noise and I will save your life from disaster. " Quick words I learned from Vidia Ercado for telling a lie that would determine truth during the time we were in the temple and still studying. We trained it two a few times until I learned to manipulate different things. I don't tell my other friends and classmates in the temple that only Vidia Ercado knows because he is my secret teacher when it comes to this nonsense. I am a disciplined person and I know it is forbidden and bad to lie but I have learned that lying can sometimes be used when you want to save someone from disaster. I don't suggest this perspective to others but this is really what I do to save others, now this is my word with certainty and I am comfortable doing it because of years and days of practice. Now I do this to get what I want and to protect myself from the caveman and boy I am talking to now who will surely die by the time I make a mistake and my tongue slips. I let out in my facial expression that I'm a little scared of telling the truth even if I'm not and because of this face of truth knowing them to feel I'm a little scared of them telling the right way is not a good option. Add to that the sweat dripping down from my face. When I was young I used to have a bit of an abnormality in my skin that made me sweat when I was scared and my brain was confused by what was currently happening.

 Danger immediately approached me and he was trying to smell the words I had left out and if it was still certain, his movements were serious and the child's weapon was ready if I added it correctly. Until he told me the word I didn't expect and the child speaking was different because of the explanations I had left to him when he told me the word I knew relates to what I had done before. "Liar, you're a lying man."

 "Liar?" I whispered back to him in support of the mistake I made, at first I was wrong because I was bored that I thought he didn't know the word Honolio.

"Honolio can't do that!" Word told me he was
sure. "I came from the temple, decades ago and I
know the goodness of Honolio." He was right,
and up to now, but when he reasoned that
decades ago, I found an opportunity to lie again.

"Yes, I know it's hard to believe but our Honolio
has changed. He is no longer the same as before
and his belief is getting worse that conquering
different areas is the way to avoid this Penac.

I saw in his eyes the annoyance and anger, I
knew he would not accept the words I had told
him concerning Honolio.

I could see in his face the frustration of what was happening in Honolio. I waited for his decision but before he could think I tried to ask if he was also one of the students of the Honolios and he insisted yes.

 "If only I and our group succeeded in finding a cure in Penac we will be able to silence this part of the place," the boy replied. Here I am wondering how this boy became a student of Honolios like me for decades. that's the past. " But how did that happen you have been a student of the Honolios for decades but you look young? "I asked him, wondering what was happening.

"I'm connected to my race." He told me that I still didn't know what was in their race and I also wanted to ask what happened to his feet but I let him speak first what he wanted to say.

 "We didn't succeed and here that I lived we failed a lot in the exam and we sacrificed our lives because of it, I was separated from my colleagues and since then I have seen this cave far away from the sick Penac and became My friend is Pathalion. (Caveman).

If I only had the Pendant I would make sure I could move. " He explained and told me a story that was somewhat similar to my experiences today.

I tried to sit and even listen to him as he walked. His stories are somewhat similar and familiar to me because I also come from his background but the old lessons contained in his stories are that I respect the old ones.

 I thought of peeing in the back first because I couldn't stop my bladder from coming out and nature would call me. While still listening to his stories maybe this is just my first plan to listen to him all day and strengthen our relationship as friends and he will help me get out of this place.

Our conversation lasted eight hours based on my hand. I learned to count time by hand from Carrin Regra when I accompanied him before in physical training and I was very tired before in that training but he told and taught me to count time by hand.

He cooked a lizard roasted on the fire from here in the cave that his friend who was a caveman had caught. I forgot the name of the caveman as he mentioned earlier.

I have never tasted a lizard in my whole life but when I was little I tried to catch a lizard to scare my young friends in the temple.

That morning I thought of visiting one of my friends and playmate Katho Don at that time he didn't know my name he always called me "Psst." when he wants to call me to play he calls me that I don't clarify his words I just let him call me that because he's a bit sharp until now.

 "What happened to your feet?" I asked the young-looking old man if he could speak. He told me that it was just an accident but he did not tell me the reason for how the accident happened. At the same time he smiled at me and I immediately asked him if he could help me with my plan and he answered that he could do nothing but follow after he warned that he handed me the grilled lizard.

At first, I didn't know what my reaction would be but I was forced to pick up and not refuse because at these times I was also hungry.

 My decision to touch and smell the grilled lizard changed that I couldn't bear to chew and eat it. I heard a noise of chewing to my right and I found an excuse to not eat what was given to my grilled lizard.

 Maybe when you are not accepted as a monk in the temple I will also learn something like this or worse there are worse foods that I have never known and seen in my whole life here out there.

I got used to eating cabbage, carrots, and normal fruits and vegetables in our temple.

I know it is wrong to compare my past world to this place but my stomach is changing.

I gave the grilled lizard to the caveman who was his companion after he finished it he immediately accepted my offer and he put out a word that I do not understand but if I relate my giving him the grilled lizard he thanked maybe to me.

But his young companion laughed at me.

There I changed and I wanted to ask the boy what the caveman told me and what he told me based on what the boy muttered was "You stupid man."

 Far from what I wanted to hear but I just let it go because it's okay for me not to eat it even if I'm hungry. Even though I'm weak, I know I'm not eating lizards.

 By the way, what happened to my childhood friend Katho Don was that while he was sleeping, a lizard suddenly entered his mouth and he did not know that he had eaten a lizard because he thought he was chocked and was suddenly accompanied by drinking water.

I laughed so hard that day that I almost fell down the wooden stairs, but I knew there was a tree blocking it and I was in a hurry to get out of there because I didn't want to be overtaken and he wondered why I was there. Every time someone comes in and I see him I can't help but laugh out loud.

So I turn around every time I see him and thankfully he doesn't notice me.

But the year passed and I forgot and I got tired of that fun but when I still remember them I just laugh like now.

The boy asked me why I was smiling but I recalled nothing and I just remembered an acquaintance who wanted to hear the story and I told him about it.

Our story lasted an additional two hours and he must have noticed what I wanted to convey to him that I was in a bit of a hurry and I needed to save their place.

"We have to walk in this direction because this is the way out." shared the boy with his caveman friend. I immediately hurried and tried to walk first with them but was told not to go first. I don't know if they noticed my lying to them at first ...

But I found out that they are good creatures and maybe after I found out and I was in the outlying area of the cave I wanted to tell them the truth.

"It's hard to know the roundabout in this area and if you're not careful and you don't follow us you'll lose a leg too so you'd better follow us." The child's advice and that I stayed behind them even though they were walking slowly and it was noticeable that the child looked like it was difficult to walk and because of this I gave my hand to help him but he refused and I just let him go instead of getting angry.

The plan to leave here was to move forward by an unspecified time because I couldn't count properly as I was walking probably just effectively counting the time I learned when sitting and doing nothing.

I followed them with only foot fire I could see it was a bit delicate in my opinion because the last time I tried to walk here in the cave I smelled oil that was sure to burn us by chance but I didn't tell them because I knew in myself that they know what they are doing and based on their experience they are the ones who made that trap.

I follow the commotion of their footsteps while only solid darkness can be seen. Suddenly I felt an insect on my face and I slapped it without knowing... it was not an insect but a small branch where the caveman was holding it so that I wouldn't get lost he began I would hold it tightly while the three of us were walking in the dark cave. I remembered the time when I'm alone at this moment when the caveman tried to kill me and now he's one of my friends who is helping and guiding me to the exit of this madness.

/ˈeldər/

We are slaves to our own decisions and misfortune.

In the dark place, danger or safety is waiting, all my plans are in line when I am left behind Henry and the caveman. Our walk lasted and I also asked his name. "Henry" his name is familiar to me but he is vaguely what I think of. Before we left the temple I met an old man named Henry, he was easily recognized by people because he was always in one place and sweeping once while I was buying a wooden sword he asked me if I liked chess. I told him before that I was a player in a temple competition. He told me that if possible we would play at least once. At first, I was a little unsure but when I saw some food on the table I was asked to give it to him a chance and my friends, they watched me fight against the old

Henry. I had strong confidence in winning but at that time the opposite happened. I was a little ashamed of my arrogance but I kept trying and asked for another fight but after that, I still lost. I didn't stop and I still tried in the third but I still didn't win him. This is where our story began my reckoning against him was hard to knock down the solid barrier to competition, I didn't budge how many times I went to him after our temple class I always went to the place of drunks because he was always there, he was really hard to beat. Our confession lasted seven years and in my whole life, I only won with him five times while I can't count how many wins he got from me. Until I heard while I was inside the temple that he was dead. I don't know how I will react to what happened but I just thought that maybe this is the time when I lose and I respect him because I didn't completely defeat him. He is my only opponent who stands out, he did not teach me to play but he made me experience the real bloody battle and until now I still have that lesson. He is one of the opponents I admire when it comes to Chess. He is the real king. So when the time of his death came I imprinted in my mind that he was King Henry the old warrior in the war when it came to chess.

 "We're close! Hold on to the rope!" Word shouted to me by young Henry in the cave.

The caveman also made noise at me but I still couldn't understand him. I wondered what language he was using to talk to Henry. Maybe a few years also used the language of the caveman during the fire all eyes. The history of burning maps everywhere has remained a mystery to me as well as to my colleagues in the temple. We don't know who and why, what caused it and how it happened. I also tried to ask our Honolios but they didn't answer us either and sometimes they just turned the conversation to another topic. They were all such excuses until we forgot and we never asked them again. Because of Penac? I don't think so.

The time runs quickly as I expected when the sound of the step of Henry and the Caveman changed a bit metallic vibrating the rhythm each clang of the step moves.I recognized that we are in the unfamiliar area of the cave and hopefully we are in the exit now.

"Wait! Do you hear that too?" I told them. While I was wondering where it was coming from I was also worried that what I was hearing was not in their plan.

"Penac. We're in!" Henry spoke to me as I heard his concern in his tone of speech and the annoyed disappointed noise of the caveman.

We immediately accelerated our run and hoped

that we would not be able to catch up with them

even though it was dark as we were walking.

We continued to run fast and confusingly. the

metal we were stepping on became quite painful

with slippery, I don't know what was sticky we

were stepping on but my knees suddenly

weakened when I asked Henry what were yours

because his answer made my stomach swell and

I stepped when he cried that they were the blood

of a dead man and the metal floor we were

stepping on was not normal metal except a thick

trap to execute anyone who tried to enter it as

well as the animals. I wondered why we had to

hurry when the defense of the cave was so

dangerous. They told me that there was a place

here with a small hole and they didn't put anything there and they were worried about that and they memorized the sounds and echoes of the cave, they knew that the sick Penac passed there in the small hole.

 While we were in a hurry I saw a chance to take a weapon I saw a pipe that I do not know what because also in the dark I deliberately got it by digging around me with my right hand while holding my left rope connected to the caveman and Henry.

 "We're close!" words Henry hesitated to me when suddenly someone attacked me from behind and hit my shoulder!

I immediately bent down and let go of the rope, I
was holding because in so much pain I saw the
disturbing noise of the Penac people behind me.
I was able to stand up and fight with them but I
was so nervous that my cowardice suddenly
increased, accompanied by the beating of my
chest with nervousness that I could no longer
swallow. I hope they don't see me in the dark. I
didn't make any noise and I don't know if my
two colleagues heard me.

 But when I saw a light not too far from my
place, I found out that they did not know that I
had let go of the rope and that turning on that
light was the reason why the Penac saw me.

I made a sharp cut at one of my oncoming

opponents and I was a little terrified by the looks

of the Penacs but I could do nothing but attack

and run because of their aggressiveness in their

movements and the trembling of anger. this is

when they touch you it is really hard to get away

and when they combine all their forces I will be

among them because with such active

movements I am sure I will be defeated if I

continue to chase them so I run just to get to the

light. I see. As I was running towards my

companions I saw the caveman rushing to where

I was running and he would try to attack the

Penacs. I tried to stop him but he just pushed

me hard Henry told me to let him go and he

showed me the way out that I could see in the

light. I asked him if he would come with me but he ignored me and he also tried to push me. A sacrifice I wanted to pay but I couldn't. I knew they were desperate to give their lives. For me? No. But for the cave. They love the cave so much that they finally don't want to leave it. I was no longer able to tell them the truth that Honolio was not ordering me to destroy their post but I thanked them at once as Henry's strong thrust rattled a rope on his left side and was suddenly covered by a thick rock cut. , the door closed and our relationship was severed.

 I tried to approach the large chunk of rock and checked if there was a way to see what was going on inside.

I saw a small hole but it was very blurry to see what was happening because it was so black and closed that no light could enter the cave. I could see but I could hear angry screams at the number of opponents, I saw inside my friends were taking their lives.

 I continued walking and I was avoiding the Penacs waiting in the cave when I saw them at the top of the cave I suddenly hid. They are at the top of the cave and waiting to see who will attack.

 What I got that I thought was a pipe in the dark cave was a sword shovel that resembled being a spear.

 A spear-sword that I knew would help me protect myself against the Penacs. But if it's against them, I'm not sure if anyone can use such a weapon. I saw an opportunity to hide in a secluded and crowded part and many types of plants and I hoped there were no snakes but here I was wrong when I saw the head of a snake when I decided to hide.

On the other side of my journey, I still tried to move here than the Penac saw me.

I had better fight the snakes and insects here in the small forest and in case they attack me I know their moves because if I go back to all our training in the temple I know their moves I know when they will attack and I know when they will leave and fear. I immediately stabbed my weapon at my stand and made a small noise that Penac could not hear but could frighten the snakes around me the signal was that I adjusted my posture with pride that I was the king and my message departed from my presence. This is the place where I can apply what I have learned in the temple. After I did this, the three snakes were removed from where I was standing but there were still less than ten left to count. ,

because maybe I'm about to starve but I'm still

standing here I thought I should just eat the

lizard and the caveman is right that I'm a fool for

not eating. But I can do nothing but continue

my mission because this is the only reason to

prevent Penac disease. I need to find my

colleagues and get out of this place. I decided

not to mess with the non-messy snakes. I look at

any angle to be active so as not to be attacked by

snakes and I also look at any fruit I can eat.

 My eyes were drawn to the grape-colored fruits

but their shape was square. They are unfamiliar

to me hanging from the trees I am also not

familiar with.

I tried to cut one with my weapon and it fell near

the snakes so I just didn't pick it up and instead I

looked for a closer fruit like the first one I saw

and I continued walking until I saw something.

I had a good place and when it fell I immediately

picked it up and cut the middle to see the inside.

It smells like an aroma that is similar to the curry

dish that our people cook in the temple but I'm

still not sure about it. I didn't want to eat poison

while I was traveling like what happened to me

in the cave so I just put the fruit in my pocket

whatever it is.

I'm not a rich and artistic person but I'm just

careful about eating what I don't know.

But after I hid the strange food I saw I saw a squirrel that also got the same fruit from me and he ate it. Suddenly his companion squirrel came and they split the fallen almost rotten fruit like mine. So I immediately took out the fruit and tried to eat it like the animals I had seen eating the same fruit I had seen. But as I expected, the taste of them turned out to be unpleasant to me. It was a bit salty when bitten, it was a bit sticky with a thick bitter taste coming out and I immediately threw it away. Perhaps this food is not human and only for the squirrels when I threw it away they hurried to go and they ate the fruit I threw away.

I took a step forward and my persistence made sense as I saw a familiar fruit as I walked. So far I have seen banana-shaped normal and no friendly texture I immediately took almost so much that I was trying to fit on each side of my fingers and I thought to sit down as I peeled them.

I was in such a hurry to eat the fruit that I was suddenly dizzy because during the time I had not eaten and my throat was dry, it was a good thing that I calmed myself down and thought that I needed to gather my sputum to push the leftover bananas. in my throat.

I felt the sting of losing the banana in my throat

so the next time I chewed it I tried a calm and

small bite while I felt like I could swallow it. In

short, I needed a pusher to stick to my throat so I

continued walking again, and hopefully, I could

find normal water here in the forest.

As I walked and ate a little, I still felt the food

stuck in my chest. I make sure my head is not

affected by dizziness with any poison I can still

balance myself.

I heard a noise and suddenly bowed because they were Penacs again. Using my weapon I was ready to attack if the opponent was alone but when they multiplied I would remain hidden while eating a banana without any water to hold and drink.

It's not amazing to think that they're not because right now I've mistakenly identified them. Someone walks like a normal person here in the forest. They're not contaminated by the Penac but their behavior is still suspicious and I didn't want to interrupt them and make a noise to scare them. But then what if they're a good person like the caveman and Henry who can help me to survive. Maybe...

Not. No way. I saw them killing each other now.

Just like they have a Penac but unrecognized

behavior to what I saw last time. They have a

Penac and not safe to be them. I hide under the

brownish big leaves that I can't say the type but

are usually good enough to hide because it's fit

to my whole body. I'm currently holding my

weapon in case they'd plan to attack or get a hint

that another living thing is hiding.

My expectation comes when they heard my foot

move a little bit closer as the cracking noise

made it loud. The one got to go slowly in my

spot as he tried to hunt me.

Hopefully, I have a tiny hole of the leaves that I can monitor what they're planning. I'm ready to attack them but waiting for the best time to show up.

/skəl/

The lesson does not end until death.

Wishing I was still with the caveman and Henry at this time.

The attack on the enemy was ready planned in my brain, but I don't think this was the time. They didn't know I was really moving or they were just imagining what they heard.

Fortunately, they are fools.

Aggressive idiots who don't know what to do, always want to kill and infect people.

I have controlled the fear and nervousness I feel, while hiding in the big leaf of not knowing what tree. Every second he slowly approached me as he separated the small plants and trees that were close to me, maybe when he saw and opened the big leaf where I was hiding. It was time to attack.

It took at least two minutes and no more than three minutes for the slowness of the Penac turtle that I wanted to kill.

Until they agree with me on what I want to happen.

He didn't see me completely but I was suddenly
shocked that he had a colleague behind me
waiting for me to move and he suddenly
attacked my back wound a bit shocked. I can't
believe that my back wound suddenly broke and
grew.

I did my best to anticipate his next attack. I
saw in his face that he was ready to kill me and I
tried to prevent the next throw with my weapon
I almost fell because of the panic I was able to
ward off but the force of his blow to me
weakened my defense. because he was able to
run solid and I was not ready for it.

I need a companion to fight them.

As I expected his other colleagues saw me.

I have little time and chance to live in this opportunity. I couldn't see my colleagues in this area.

It is also impossible for me to survive.

Emily, the old woman told me that I had to face death without fear and apprehension. When I was young he told me how short life is. Emily was the old woman who made me feel sad and beware of death.

As I was unleashing the blows and scratches on me by the Penac, his presence in the background suddenly appeared in my imagination. Maybe my time is near and maybe all I can do is fight the Penacs to my death.

  The falling trees and squirrels I had seen before were gone. The Penac creatures came to my place when I couldn't measure how many they had and they only had one plan.

  They were all staring at me.

  I can't swallow properly because maybe it's the cold around me and I'm a little confused because they keep multiplying.

I kept pulling out my slow-moving weapon to find a new strategy to escape as I found a path that I could defeat.

I don't see where to go because its lands are quite high compared to where we stand. Small mountains in comparison and quite a distance if I go slowly. With the blade of my spear sword the Penacs are becoming a bit smarter because of the few times I cut their skins but when they find the opportunity it is also the time of my death.

I was no longer able to count my footsteps in

the event now it was a bit unlikely I could even

breathe properly because they were afraid of the

sword I was holding I tried to speed it apart

from them. I looked a bit dangerous at the first

attempts to approach me but my path was

narrow so I thought of changing the angle of our

direction as I protected my own life with the

spear sword I saw in the cave.

I'm not intimidated by their cries but ...

I felt death calling to me as they tried to attack

me at the same time.

It was time to run on the right side where there was no Penac and I was running uphill but when I got to the end I saw the high cliff and the landing. The rest of my chance was lost when I saw the sharp molds of the woodland on the chin and I saw drops of blood I didn't know where it came from.

I have already decided.

May my comrades be safe and may their mission to prevent Penac be successful.

I wish I had spent a long time with Henry and Emily.

But I was determined to get to this point and my life was happy somehow. Although I did not stay long in the Woil West Temple, the lessons I learned there became my lifelong and in the end.

But there is one last thing I want to do before my life ends.

Count how many Penac I can defeat with my spear-sword.

I went to a good place because the ground I was treading was uphill.

I started being a warrior in my tenth year,
when I was young I thought I was a king of the
kingdom I was protecting against evil people. I
rush with dignity and courage over every
obstacle and my attack will knock down the
opponents because I am a strong man. It is not
easy to fall because I am part of nature that
protects the world. The courage that lingers in
my heart is unforgivable because my principles
are straightforward and high. Resistant even to
death. My name stands out only because I have
a strong stand.

Lion is my eye and my heart is diamond.

My Mathala's advice…

Go! It's time to ignite;

Turn down the fright;

Your keen eyes bright;

Everything is alright.

I felt her touch my face. While fighting the

Penac I had felt the caress of the being I loved. I

know this event is just my imagination but this

is how it feels while fighting death.

You will remember the people you love.

My Rebecca was the woman I loved outside the temple, a time when I could still see the beauty outside. Rebecca was the girl I met at a time when the water in the creek was dirty and when I saw her beautiful face the call of my heart was revived. I felt love for a woman and since our Honolio decides who we love I can insert the story of the woman Rebecca in my Honolio and I am happy to see the face of our Honolio because like me he is also a man who falls in love with the beautiful young lady. We talk to our dear women when we have the time and opportunity to talk in the temple. I agree with the old man Honolio so he was very sad that I could not pass the tests.

This is the time when I need to say goodbye.

They bit me on the hand, shoulder, and on any
part of my face as well as on parts of my body
that I did not know why they were biting.

I felt the rapid swelling of my hands and also the
crash of my brain and heart changed. As they
continued to bite I became more and more
different from everything I could no longer
control my toes, as well as my knees, and half
my body was weakening because of the bites.

This is the Penac I felt that they were different from everyone else. My strength was sinking and my eyes were only wide open while I was still moving my eyes I remained wide open and awake to the events I still wanted to see before I was deprived of life.

I heard and even saw the second, I let go of my spear-sword.

And here my life ended.

****

I heard the strange noise and annoying sound of the animal that I knew what ... chickens.

Suddenly I jumped up and ran so fast that I didn't know what that feeling was that lingered in my physical body. There is no fun and I want to cry or laugh but I can't control my cheeks and teeth. I heard the chickens again and I was so annoyed with them that I went to them one by one and killed them. I wasn't like this before ... Before?

I don't remember the previous ones. I am thirsty and hungry.

Why is there a spear-sword here? What is my personality? Why do I have black hands that if I move are like rough wood and a bit itchy?

I also noticed that I was quickly irritated by the crackles around me. My eyes are very sharp and I can see even small objects, as well as the noise of ants and insects, walking I also quickly know and I have a very bad headache.

I feel like I'm going to faint that I can't pass out. It was as if I was floating that I was not floating. Feeling that running is not tiring and lifting growing broken trees.

I want to speak properly but I can't and only different noises come out of my mouth.

"Penac." Word I'm not sure where it comes from.

"You're already one of us." I looked around again and in the distance from my seat, I saw people like me with strange hands and heads. Even in the distance, they can be heard and I know who is speaking.

"We are the modern people. Don't be afraid, because we are the ones they should fear. You are already one of us, Penac calls us and we need to consume the races of mortals. They need to wake up to the truth. They need a new evolution like us. " Word he says to me in the distance.

Now I understand everything. I know I used to be human but I can't remember my name.

In the distance of my destination, I could still

hear the voice of a creature that I wanted to

attack and bite.

I was in a hurry to go to whatever it was I knew

it was coming from the cave.

I could not feel that I was breathing, creatures

like me were moving fast behind me.

They are just as irritable as I am. We agree with

what we want to do as we all jump pretty

smoothly and our faces are aggressive when we

hear mortals all of a sudden I can't control my face to be actively wanting to attack always wherever I am irritated. I just felt it for the first time but I seem to know why I feel it.

"Let go of your body, it will move spontaneously because you are different now." Words warned to me by a creature like me not far away were understood and I could still hear him.

"How do I do this?" I asked him and many replied, "Just, just let it do what you want to do!"

I was confused, I couldn't understand them all as we ran towards the cave our actions were almost the same and I understood their words.

We got inside the cave as I followed my fellow

Penacs who were ahead of me and both of us

wanted to attack. I don't know why but this is

what my body says I need to bite them. I don't

understand what mortals are saying but they

look familiar to me. His feet looked like a child

of wood and I could see a large monkey-like

creature. My ear gets irritated when they talk, I

don't know why, but it's like I added bite them.

My teeth came out of my mouth and I couldn't

control them I turned to people like me they

were so well that I pretty much couldn't explain

what was currently happening to us and why

we wanted to bite them. Suddenly my former

companion rushed at them and was suddenly chased away by a large creature comparable to a monkey with a thick stack of sticky wood.

Suddenly another colleague of mine rushed at them again but his whole body was burned with one I could not determine the mystery or magic the boy used on him.

All my fellow Penac rushed at them and I was the only one left not because I was trying to understand everything even though I wanted to bite them. I'm still enduring it somehow but it seems like my head hurts more no matter what I do to stop them I still want to bite them and at this time it's the same that they Penac me with an itchy thing on my back and I feel hairy. I kept holding and I reached for them but I had nothing to hold on to.

"Attack them! If you want to survive!" They told me.

"I don't want," I answered them ... I knew I was irritated and I wanted to bite them but I couldn't.

"You'll die if you don't bite them!" Penac people like me say.

"I don't care!" I answer them. Repeated sounds of shaking metal and glass I could hear but I was not irritated by it because my ear was more annoyed by the breathing of the two mortals among us.

All those itching behind me who are also like me Penac are coming to attack the two people in the middle. I'm the only one who doesn't.

"You're just like us! Attack them to keep you alive! Everyone who can't bite mortals is dying!" begged my colleague Penac to me as he tried to attack the two people.

I want to get rid of my itching and irritation with mortals but I don't want to do it because I don't want to be bitten by a mortal because I know I used to be mortal.

I could hear the fluttering of butterflies on my unspecified part and I noticed there was trickling water in front of me. I peed.

My Penac colleagues saw this and they immediately did not look at me. But because of this, the itching of my foot has somewhat disappeared with the flow of urine on my foot. So I thought of lying down and soaking my whole body in it.

Gradually the itching disappeared but the longing to bite the mortal did not go away. As my Penac peers continued to rush at the two people fighting for their lives it was that I remained stunned by them while lying in the water I urinated on to relieve the irritation.

Penac people like me told me I was crazy but I didn't pay attention to them.

My hands started to tremble and I stood up because I couldn't control my feet and I wanted to scratch mortals but I was still trying to control this temptation.

/sən/

Morning is dark to the person without a smile.

I remember the morning of the past. As well as

the darkness of every problem, I solved while I

was here in the monster state.

 Go back to my memory of the temple from

which I came. The mission.

 My former colleagues put forth they were

holding the Pendant. I immediately saw and

remembered the young-looking Henry and the

caveman in front of me. I don't know if they still

know me but I think it's vague because I look

different and based on the past I can no longer

speak the language of mortals.

The chance sided with us when I saw in my eyes that Henry had slipped. While the webs man was busy exchanging attacks, he didn't notice Henry needing help. My fellow Penacs found an opportunity to quickly attack them.

My former colleagues and I mistakenly thought that Penac patients were killing. Instead, they all work together to attack mortals.

I have experienced being them.

It was so hard to resist the temptation to bite a mortal while I was under Penac disease.

I moved my feet again at a pace I had never

experienced running in my entire life as a Penac

before. I immediately went and struck hard

with my immeasurable courage and my anger at

Penac who wanted to attack Henry.

"What is the meaning of this!" Angry words

that the Penac man told me that I would almost

be killed by the blow of my anger towards him.

"Don't bite them!" Words stand out only anger I

let out at them as I prepared to protect Henry

against them.

I never thought Henry would ever recognize me,
this time I still knew my real opponent and that
was them! My Penac colleagues. I started to
jump slightly to prevent and defend their next
attack.

 It brings back to my memory almost all the
events I want to remember.

 Marlen Balas's nervousness and joy when I tell
her about the invented stories are what the
Penac are. Even though he is old, he still likes to
listen to all my stories, even the untrue things I
told him that he believes.

Legar Velma being a friendly man to all my colleagues and also to me I can't imagine when we started to be friends because to the extent of his imagination, many times we make decorations whenever there are good contests in the temple. Legar Velma is the one I can say sleepy and shy because he always finds it hard to talk to a lot of people and I notice he wants to change the ugliness of his habit. He was thin so I could easily push him to the women he used to flirt with.

When it comes to selfishness, Yora Dence's behavior is unforgivable. inhabited by his members but Katho Don saw and rebuked him for his selfishness. I also don't quite understand Katho Don's actions before because of being a rude member of ours and maybe that's also the reason because he also didn't pass the test like me. He has a different attitude towards Marlen Balas even though they are the same age, Marlen's goodness still stands out compared to Katho.

What Rion Hein told me came back to me that he wanted to live up to his expectations, he was also a bit fat like me, and a few times my brother and I had been mistaken for the temple.

He was happy to be alone and sometimes I accompanied him mesmerized by the plants while sitting alone in the garden of our Honolio. Nor can he be bargained for in creating a work that in half a minute he can impress everyone because of his talent in drawing and I admit that he should be known in the temple as a masterpiece like Legar Velma.

 I suddenly smiled as I remembered the embarrassment done by Sealo Wise, the man who was afraid of ghosts.

Skinny and not blessed with a stature like Yora Dence but in character is different because he had a ghost story in the temple when we were able to frighten him that night when our Honolio ordered him to guard the courtyard of the temple door decided Legar Velma and I made a fool of him. We startled him when we dropped the curtain on top and we made a scary noise so that he could run away.

 The next morning he told us about his experience and we all laughed, then he realized and promised us that he would take revenge for what happened to his cowardice he made us all laugh that it reached the Honolios and made everyone laugh at him.

Until he felt embarrassed so he didn't want to

talk to us because of that.

 Morally I admire Carrin Regra she is the same

man as me who proved that everyone should be

disciplined and plan our actions because of this I

admire her because as far as I know, she was my

childhood.

I learned from him being responsible and

helping the weak before there was a mess

opposite where I was sleeping he was near the

tree to observe the fight between the old man

and the soldier in the temple he immediately

took action and went to the fight, he suddenly

jumped in the middle and he stopped the soldier

because he was going to try to push the old man.

We didn't like the soldier because of this, we knew he was new but he also needed to know that we were new to him because first of all we treated him well but when we found out and saw what he did to the old man it was I immediately became angry because of his actions. After Carrin Regra came down he was our male leader at a time when someone was oppressed he always took action and we followed as his backup in battle.

 Maybe among those I knew in the temple, there was one I didn't trust and that was Brane Yares the man like me who could annoy everyone because of his cursed words.

He is our leader in the temple but no one wants

him to be a leader because of his behavior that is

commanded and you think he is a black king

who walks and tortures slaves. Our Honolio

also criticized him several times for his behavior

like this but no change has come to the point that

until now we do not like his behavior. I

remember the time he became the leader and all

of us members of the temple wanted him to

leave and expel because he was giving us a

dangerous mission that we had to finish just like

killing snakes and getting the old lion's fang. in

the woods than that we had not yet been

expelled from the temple. We didn't follow his

silly ones instead of listening to him we made a

new group and we separated him from us until

he realized and I saw in his eyes that he wanted

to retaliate because of it but he could do nothing.

He took a boulder and threw it at all of us.

Fortunately, we were ready to avoid it and no

one was hit or hurt when he threw a large rock.

He got as far as our Honolio where he lost his

teammates. I can't remember the reason why we

included him in the group and we were just

forced because our Honolio told us that we were

still in the group and he apologized to us before

but his eyesight and tone of his speech still

smelled bad.

 Mockie Genole, on the other hand, is the shield-

loving man without a weapon.

He was a tall and thin man who always proved himself faithful to the principle of temple discipleship. One day I was walking to the temple courtyard and would have arranged the glued chairs and would have swept because the celebration of the new Honolio in the temple had just ended when I saw him earlier than me and he started to do it. the jobs he doesn't have to do. To my surprise, the chairs were also clean and free of dust or dirt stains. I wanted to ask why he was doing this but he preceded me in saying that I would just thank him. It is his job to fix the things he sees that are not pleasing to his eyes. From then on, when he was tidying up and doing something clean, I let him eat even though I was the one ordered by Honolio. He was not fond of recognition and several times he refused the awards given to him because he believed Ray was not the measure of being a good person.

Mockie was the true shield of the temple as we heard that he freed the secret slaves of the temple officials.

The news I received came only from the letters of truth I read every morning. The role of the true story is given to all of us who attend the temple, every morning we receive news.

I was shocked that Mockie Genole turned out to be the content of the first true story in the paper given to me. So I immediately read the words contained here and hope I can read good news about him also because I know he deserves them for the good things he did that we admire.

 In the news that night, Mockie tried to find out the secret tunnel under the house near the temple. He broke every thin iron-like cage built for the people.

In the darkness of the surroundings, he lit his lamp with the small fire he had made with matches. Here he witnessed small children being held by their parents' ns bent over and he wondered what they were doing here under the houses the man distributed that they were just some of the slaves who had not paid taxes and they had to pay for it with their service. The slaves wore a twisted cloth and placed it on their heads as a symbol that they were slaves for the life of the officers. This news is a bit unfair because it has spread as far outside the Woil West Temple as before. Many starve under the dungeon of slaves and many also die from overwork and dust or dirt with them in their dungeons. According to the slaves, they also thought of running away several times but they were killed one by one because of it. Mockie became their hero and according to the news he was almost killed when someone suddenly stabbed his soldier with a big knife, it went straight to his chest and fortunately, he always wore a shield that protected him from harm, and because of this, he was constantly at odds. The slaves supported him because Mockie promised them at those times that Mockie would use this iron hand the first time he did. Because based on my mind it was Mockie who made peace when we were young and we were quite old in the temple at that time it is here in the news I read that he killed an evil soldier. After I read this I immediately got suited and ate to see how one of my friends Mockie was doing right now.

I walked a few minutes and went back to the places my friend Mockie always went to. I didn't see him in the area of the gardens that I once always saw him in before cleaning. They didn't even have the energy they used to have and there was garbage so it was obvious that Mockie was no longer cleaning this place. I continued walking quickly and tried to go to the small market near the temple.

It also lost its vitality and many people there were also wondering like me where Mockie was, his former position was now vacant and the knife he used to cut off the heads of tuna fish from outside the Woil West Temple was standing.

He does this every morning but he doesn't have any traces and equipment in the market. the elders asked me where he was and I told them that I also didn't know anything.

I no longer tell them what I heard in the fact paper that is given to us every morning because I don't want the story to grow that my friend Mockie was murdered. After I passed the market I remembered another place he went to and that was our Honolio farm to feed the chickens raised by the Woil West Temples that could not be slaughtered.

We raise chickens at the Woil West Temple because we already believe it gives us prosperity.

We do not kill animals other than fish. But I was very sad when I got to the farm and saw a lot of chicken blood scattered around and many dead people here.

Suddenly I heard a quick and loud throw of the spear on my left side and here I saw the sad face and posture of my friend Mockie.

"What are you doing here?" he asked me. I did not answer but I approached him.

"Don't come near me!" He warned as he explained that he was a dangerous person and that he could no longer do what he used to do. He felt that he was a strange person.

As I talked to him I could see in his eyes the anxiety and fear in me as I continued to approach him he also continued to walk away. "Are you the reason the chickens died?" I asked him as Mockie looked at his hands and deeply told me that ...

"I didn't do that, they were knocked down by a wall that fell last night because of the earthquake."

"I'm not the same as I am right now, Leodor," He stated to me he sobbed. I told him that what happened to the news is not his fault but he regretted that was his mistake.

He mention that he can't control his anger at that time because he was passionate to help the slaves.

"But you completely protected them!" I insist on him and he replied " Yeah, by killing a guard."

"A bad guard," I replied.

"But he's still a person." He cried and I didn't respond because he knew that when you kill a person it's unforgivable sin in the temple.

" I don't know what's happening to me. Yesterday I was a knight but now I'm a killer.

I guess this is my fate, Leodor." He ventured while he was lying on the grass.

"What's your feeling right now?" I asked him as I sit beside him.

"I'm very sad, my responsibility to protect people is to die." He countered.

/ˈēvniNG/

The night is a symbol of rest to the good person.

"All the news about you is right?" I asked him as he lay and looked at the clouds.

 "Yes, I didn't mean, but I did." He answered my question. I know that he did not mean what happened but his conscience continues to envelop him and does not silence him so that he can't breathe completely from what happened.

 The night they happened even the slaves I rescued also saw the death of the guard. Even they were amazed at what I had done and even I did not know if I should still be here in the Woil West Temple.

I also don't have to protect the chickens that are here, maybe this is the end of my responsibility. I just deserve to be kicked out of the temple.

"But our Honolio isn't letting you go," I answer to his misdeeds in life that he has to go on or forget to feel guilty because I know there is nothing too bad there. He helped the slaves he freed. I don't know if he listens to what I'm saying and isn't sure what he should do because he shows no willingness to listen. My view of my friend also changed. I accompanied him at those times I saw our Honolio time he also saw me and approached me. While Mockie still has a shield it is no longer worn by him.

Our Honolio was walking and he found Mockie's shield. He walked over to us and told me how my fellow knight was doing. I replied to my Honolio that his principle was wounded. He asked if I was his friend and I nodded at his question.

"We will be punished." our Honolio suddenly amplified his word so that Mockie could hear them. I was also surprised by Honolio's opening remarks that he usually did not say these words to all his former students. Suddenly Mockie stood up lying on the grass as if all these events were natural to him.

"I hope so, what punishment I deserve." My
friend replied to our Honolio that he seemed to
have no fear and emotion in his face.

Our Honolio threw Mockie's shield at him.

"Put that on again. Come to me at the door of
our temple and there you will know your
punishment." After our Honolio hissed these
words he proceeded to turn away and walk
toward the temple.

As for Mockie he picked up his shield and tried to put it on again. Suddenly our Honolio stopped walking as if he had forgotten to say something but for a second he resumed walking. He suddenly called my name and told me that if I wanted to go with Mockie I would go to him too. Mockie warned me not to obey because he didn't want help with the punishment to be given to him but I had a conscience before, he took on my responsibilities before which he did without my permission.

 I told him that he could do nothing because our Honolio also invited me and I decided to help him with his punishment that I knew this punishment was very heavy.

But if my life is to be the substitute it is good to
listen to the story of the fact that I supported the
hero Mockie because of this punishment
awaiting him.

 Mockie and I waited for half a minute for
Honolio to say at the temple door. There were
many people there waiting just like us who were
keeping in touch with what was going to happen
while Mockie was seriously looking deep into
the ground and I was imitating him but I was
looking at the walking ants in only one direction
while listening to the different ones. Another
word I can't understand that comes from
everyone watching us.

They were wondering why I was included to be punished like Mockie but I heard our step Honolio and he clarified that I was not at fault but I volunteered to help Mockie with his punishment. My classmates who were also watching and our Honolio whispered to us the punishment awaiting Mockie as well as me.

We had to live in the Deltor Museum for two weeks.

The Deltor Museum is known as the place of corpses. I hope that things will be this bad because of my friend's sin, but I will not complain about helping a heroic friend of mine, Mockie, in his mission.

The Deltor Museum is a place that cannot be measured centuries ago but he has stood since he was a child the oldest person here in our temple. In my whole life, I have never been there and maybe everyone here at Woil West Temple like me has never been there that only my friend and I will experience the mystery event whatever is contained therein the Deltor Museum we will both know.

The Deltor Museum stands outside the Woil West Temple high. My friend and I went down as our Honolio showed us the way, he accompanied us to immediately trace the Deltor Museum area and he gave advice that we both be careful.

Mockie walked first while wearing his shield but as like as before he didn't have a weapon in his hand. We started walking and our Honolio looked at me, I nodded to him after that he walked back to the temple and I followed my friend.

I thought of picking up the pretty tree trunks I could use to whip up any creatures we might encounter. Our first walk was successful because it was a bit smoky. After all, it was in an old place that had long been inaccessible to the friendly smell of dust and old walls.

I tried to touch the door of the Deltor Museum because Mockie and I had to open it to get inside. Mockie told me I don't have to do this and I replied to him that you don't have to say that either and he laughed at me and told me stupid.

We saw the inside and I was amazed at the sheer size of its scope that seemed even wider than the entire Woil West Temple, the area Mockie and I were seeing. We heard noises we didn't know what, but if I was to be asked it was the sounds of bats or rats I heard and not the voices of creatures that would kill us. I was amazed at the sheer size of the Deltor Museum and even Mockie was.

We thought of walking slowly. With every step, we take it creates a very noisy sound that echoes all around the courtyard. I was a little nervous when the door we opened suddenly closed and I tried to go back but it closed completely and signaled that we were confined to the Deltor Museum.

 "That's fourteen more days to open," Mockie told me as I tried to hang with my friend again. We're both inedible and I'm not prepared for what might happen. I'm also sure there's nothing to eat in this place.

The Deltor Museum was full of paints and pictures and I tried to avoid and not touch them because it was too dusty and I didn't know how long the dust had been here. We continued walking my friend. The surroundings are dark and the high windows do not see the sun but we can see so well that I can't determine which direction the light is coming from which helps us see the different kinds of masterpieces that I have only seen in my whole life...

"The light came from the edges of the work"
Mockie explained to me as if he already knew
and memorized this place so I asked him why
and how he found out. He answered my
question and snapped that the book came from
his knowledge.

 I remember the book to the Deltor Museum was
in our library before. I also tried to see that book
before but our Honolio banned us and placed
the book at the top of the books signaling that
we are not allowed to read and touch that book
because it carries a maledictions.

We just had fun telling that story and I also don't know if it's true that the book has a imprecations so I wonder how Mockie read the book yet it is forbidden to read it in our library room. He told and explained to me that he was able to read it before being banned from reading the book and Mockie told me that the book is not cursed because that place where the book is focused is cursed and we are here with the hoodoo itself. "It's a place of greedy and sinful people who have sinned. I don't know why it's here at the Deltor Museum." explanation and Mockie told me.

Suddenly my stomach hurt I told this to my friend Mockie and suddenly the shape of his face changed. What's going on in your face? I asked Mockie. I felt like I was in magic that I didn't fully understand. I could hear Mockie asking what was happening to me as I tried to close my eyes open to see Mockie's face clearly but I couldn't do it. "I think, I'm dizzy!" I shared to Mockie. I held my friend's hand because I couldn't stand up properly. I heard in my ear the words "Innocent! To me is your soul!" a lot of people tell me words I don't understand and I don't want to hear and I'm a little scared because what I've heard is true and fortunately Mockie took away the smoke that was approaching us and that's why it was called the evil eye of this place.

 I thanked Mockie and thankfully he is knowledgeable in this area. Mockie advised me not to approach the smoke because my mind was too dangerous and what I saw here was so scary that I knew in the end that was what would kill us. I asked Mockie what to call those smokes and he told me it was one of those 'Hell Dusts' that when you are in smoke you will see illusion creatures and you can't think of them as illusions because they are so real and they are realistic.

After Mockie told the story and his explanation about Hell Dust I just followed in his footsteps. I have seen beautiful works of people playing kite painted and people at war. Each painting engraved in the museum contains stories when I saw the costume of the former Honolio that was also painted. Mockie and I stopped walking when we saw what the former Honolio looked like I didn't know what the name was.

 But I think Mockie knew who this Honolio man was, so I asked him if he knew it and he told me that he had forgotten the name of Honolio but he knew what he did just like he killed him off the man and he painted his face while he was here.

I also heard that he has never been back to the temple and until now is blank in the book of the Deltor Museum which is now the ancient Honolio we see. Mockie explained to me as I listened to him. It is easy to say that we see a Honolio because from the beginning they have the same fabric and style of clothing. The red cloth is always on the shoulders and the black is on the whole body with a white round cloth at the waist and white round cloth placed at the elbows.

We continued to walk and discover things we wanted to see and both Mockie and I were fascinated by everything we saw, the sheer extent of our surroundings inside the Deltor

Museum we weren't even halfway through and

missing the whole day or three days to reach or

visit all around us. I pretty much haven't

measured how, and how many days we'll be

able to go in full. Because some of the stairs

Mockie and I see and walk are a bit old and close

to breaking. Surely the ones we were looking for

in other parts of the Deltor Museum were close

to breaking when we tried two more back we

knew they were sinking.

 Mockie and I decided to stop in the middle of

the room and he told me he needed to rest here

in the place where we were standing.

He started to sit in the middle and I observed

our surroundings to see if it was safe and there

was no Hell Dust in the area. It was Mockie who

seemed to be afraid of him. Mockie's ability to

be like this is amazing and I'm also here so I

asked him how he was afraid of Hell Dust

coming at him and the time they covered my

whole body was how he was not affected by the

illusion and told me Mockie that he also didn't

know what was going on.

 He closed his eyes and told me to sleep like him

too because his end had come.

I don't understand what he's saying but I think he's trying to say goodbye but I haven't been able to make it clear yet because this is how my friend used to speak.

After Mockie was able to rest, we toured our next destination inside the Deltor Museum, just like before, Hell Dust is still all around us. Fortunately, Mockie was able to scare them. We saw different kinds of work as the previous giant people in the picture I saw. Next, Mockie rested again because it was noticeable that he was tired from our walk, even though it seemed like we would be able to go to all the places here, but I still waited for him to rest and I also felt hungry.

After a few minutes of his rest, we finally resumed walking to see the next one we should see old pictures -fashioned still in our eyes the works.

Just like what happened before, we are still surrounded by Hell Dust.

Midway through the end of our trip inside the Deltor Museum Mockie stopped to walk.

"The time has come my friend, goodbye Leodor," Mockie told me, and eventually, his body changed and turned into smoke. I was suddenly startled and backed away by the smoky Mockie moving quickly towards the door we came from to enter here in the Deltor Museum and he opened the door loudly and again I heard all kinds of noise in the room even the Hells Dust and Mockie's smoke eventually disappeared.

That's what my friend Mockie was letting go of.

I walked in and out of the Woil West Temple and I didn't know that fourteen days had passed since then.

I didn't tell our Honolio what happened because he didn't want to hear it and told me to keep it to myself and not tell others what happened to the hero Mockie Genole. News of the truth spread the day I returned to the temple and he was on the first page that Mockie was dead.

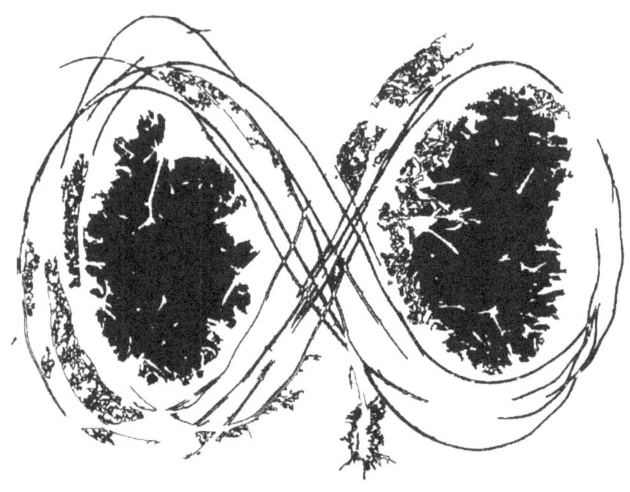

/inˈsefələn,enˈsefəlän/

Even if we pick up lessons from others, we will

not be able to get their mastery.

Also a few years ago I almost forgot about my friend Mockie.

I just remember Henry throwing a bomb around us with enormous smoke coming out of our place.

Henry and the caveman set many traps in the cave. I try to be firm in protecting them and I am ready to attack Penacs, like me every second and hour. I almost control my teeth, I can't imagine why I get mad at mortals and what kind of desire it is to bite human flesh.

When I feel I need to bite humans I suddenly

walk away from them and as I watch they attack

Henry and the Cave people I don't notice that

they think of me the same as my peers that I

know if I put myself in them of course only. I

have no difference in the physical characteristics

of the Penac the difference is ...

"Why are you attacking us!" my colleague asked

me who also like Penac. I told him not to attack

mortals and they would not listen to me and

they would continue to attack.

I feel like my sharp nails are getting a little tired

and my shoulders are weakening with the

thickness of my attack on Penac like me.

I didn't feel tired at first but after a few hours of attacking Penac like me, I could feel the weakness of my shoulders and hands. Maybe the time has come for ... For me to be bitten by a mortal! I immediately started Henry.

I still remember everything I knew we Penacs were evil but I felt I needed to bite mortals. Suddenly my teeth came out and a trembling jaw made me feel anxious to be bitten by a mortal. I couldn't understand what Henry was saying to his fellow caveman. I'm sure they plan to attack and kill me too but I want to get bitten.

My actions I can no longer control are probably right Penac likes me that even if I don't do anything my body willfully will take action to bite the mortal. I feel my bones growing in my back unlike the Penac ones I see as I attack them, Henry, I want to apologize and make me cry as I attack my mortal friends. I unleashed a powerful blow into Henry's face and fortunately, he broke it with his weapon which was quite strong as I tried to weigh down my fists and Henry was still able to defend them. Now after I did this, my left hand reached out to attack the caveman who was protecting Henry, and fortunately, he had a big hammer and small sharp thorns and he caught me in the face and stopped me, attack the two of them.

This is what I want to happen, it's okay for them
to kill me than for me to bite them.

I lied to them and I failed my mission as they
did. Henry reminded me of Mockie my friend
who risked his life to save me.

Those times used to be. I know that Mockie
already knew that he was going to say goodbye
and at that time when we entered the Deltor
Museum, the malediction had already begun.
Mockie saved me because of Hell Dusts he
became a Hell Dust too.

After I visited the Deltor Museum I found out that there was no curse on the book in the library room so I ran away and I secretly took the book regarding the Deltor Museum and I ran it to my Honolio and I didn't show and quintet what I did to the like my student.

I found out in the book that I could still talk to my friend.

Mockie.

"It's your time. How are you traveling friend ..."

I could hear Mockie's voice in my ear. Mockie?

"Yeah, I'm sorry I didn't tell you right away that I was going to let you know when we were just entering the Deltor Museum."

I also read the book. I ran away from that after I got stuck in the Deltor Museum.

"You know everything. You know I was almost tempted to take your innocent soul."

Yes, but until the end, I still salute you for what you did.

"You'll be with me in a few minutes."

I know ... I read that reference in the book too.

"Do what you have to do, friend. I'll be back to you shortly."

I nodded at him.

****

I saw Henry and the caveman trying to leave the cave but my desire to bite them grew even though my hands and feet were weakening from attacking them.

I can't even attack Penac people like me and they just watch me weaken while they give all their strength to bite Henry and the caveman but they can't do anything because the defense of the two against them is strong.

There were many traps that the two of them had set in the cave and they knew the ins and outs even in dark places. Just now I also saw that Henry was very brutally attacking the Penac and he was just like the caveman. I noticed farther and farther away between me and my companions and I had a strange smell around the dark cave. The flame and smoke are my ends.

Suddenly my surroundings caught fire.

"It's time, friend"- Mockie.

"Finally ... I'll see the truth too"- Leodor.

"Leodor, what do you want to know?" -Mockie.

"Whose necklace is that?"-Leodor.

"The necklace story isn't true. My dad just did it
to sacrifice people like you."-Mockie.

"Your father is our Honolio?" I was surprised at
what I heard.

Suddenly my surroundings changed and all of a sudden I went to the Deltor Museum as before and I saw the image of Mockie in the works. I knew I had been in the cave lately and suddenly I was just here with my old friend Mockie. I no longer hear Mockie's voice at these times.

"What do you mean the Pendant is just a trap, Mockie ?! Why does our Honolio have to do this ?!"

But I heard no voice and I am now confined to the Deltor Museum.

***

The spread of the Penacs progressed and the necklace was still carried by the remaining failed people who previously lived in the Woil West Temple.

I'm Marlen Balas. One of my friends and colleague here on my mission, Leodor Bumb, has been missing for a few days. My body also hurts because I'm probably getting older and maybe in a few days I won't be able to survive the relentless attacks on us by the Penac. I was also isolated from the rest of our colleagues whose names I didn't know very well.

Fortunately, Katho Don was with me on the trip even though I didn't like his attitude and Rion Hein very much. I also spent a few days with them on this mission. I have the Pendant, Legar Velma gave it to me when we are running.

Every day we had to prepare food, we also heard that the Penacs only attack when it is close tonight and at night itself. So we were safe in the morning we were also not sure because there were crazy people who believed that Penac was a hoodoo and they had to sacrifice human life in the place we went we were also keeping these crazy people away. We also moved around the hiding place because the weather was getting colder and we needed to keep warm. I'm used to cold places but my nose is so sensitive that it usually can't stand the cold and I suddenly sneeze. It's cold and windy where we're staying now and I don't have blankets and wraps all over my body to keep warm a little. So did Rion and Katho. We didn't know if we would continue the mission because the mission was so dangerous and so difficult that we had to finish it.

"Do you remember when one of our colleagues went to the Deltor Museum when we were still in the Woil West Temple?" Rion told us as I warmed my body by rubbing my hand and creating a warm hand plaster on my cold knees because we are getting older too.

"Yes, Leodor Bumb? Did he used to be with ... Mockie? Did I mention the name correctly?" I asked Rion again.

He nodded at me. I asked him why he asked and he stated he just remembered those.

We went back to our hand-warming routines and applied them to various parts of our cold bodies.

"Aren't we leaving yet?" Katho Don asked us that we know that he is a little annoyed and irritated because of the time we sat and we are not progressing, it is difficult to move forward when we are lacking and I have the key to success.

"What's your plan?" Rion Hein asked, knowing that he was also annoyed by Katho Don's mouth and the irritating tone of his speech, which he complained about every day.

"Why don't we just go there?" Katho Don replied while pointing at the big roof of the building that I know...

According to the Deltor Museum. Not too far from our place.

I knew that place was also dangerous and I told them that what Katho Don was planning to go to was more dangerous than the place where we were.

"What are you up to? We're going to die here?"
Katho Don asked us which I think is more okay
than his plan.

"We have to wait for our colleagues," Rion
answered Katho Don's question.

"What if they're dead and we're the only three
left on this mission," Katho grumbled angrily to
Rion.

"Do you still have a good idea that Marlen and I will get along ?!" Rion also responded angrily to Katho while I was just listening to the pointless argument because they couldn't do anything but follow me, I had the Pendant that our Honolio gave us.

"Give me the Pendant and let me lead this mission!" shouts Katho tells us that I think it's a bad idea because Kathy's arrogance has no destination and it would be even crazier if the Pendant went to him.

"All right, give him the Pendant! Marlen." Rion says angrily to me because he is now sending out angry emotions at Katho.

"Nope," I replied to the two of them that only

our fellow members would decide to whom the

pendant would go. "I know you're just

following the law given to us by Honolio. But

you can trust me if you give me the Pendant.

We've been looking for a place to go for a few

days now and we've eaten up the food we stole

from the trees and everywhere. , now that our

colleagues are gone, give me a chance to lead

these things for at least one day. should. Give

me a day and I will not disappoint you two with

the plans I have in mind.

Rion Hein looked at me to see if I would agree with what Katho Don sobbed. I know Katho is a bit bad but he is strong and I think nothing bad will happen and he promised that's he will not disappoint us so I told him that I will give him one day when we don't like him I will take back the key immediately when we know that our lives are in danger because of the decisions he will make. I took the pendant out of my pocket and my hands were also a bit shaking due to old age and I didn't like the cold I was experiencing.

I gave Katho Don the necklace.

"Come on, hurry up, we have to leave." The naughty Katho Don told us that there seemed to be a plan to put us in danger even though we didn't know what he was thinking and he hadn't shouted yet he suddenly took the pendant, and suddenly we and he left his used trash in his chair and he invited us to leave.

"Where are you going to kill us?" Rion asked Katho if he was able to attack the mad Katho with a joke while I was having trouble standing up because of my age.

I'm not as strong as I used to be because I get
sick every day when I move. Maybe it was just a
coincidence that I ran too fast and I was with
two of my colleagues at the time when we were
all still complete. May no one die and be
dumbfounded by what they saw here outside
the Woil West Temple.

Katho pointed to where the three of us were
going and pointed his finger at what I expected
of his dangerous plan and that was to go to the
Deltor Museum.

We walked and the sun was still a bit clear but we could hear the crackling of windows in every house we passed and someone showed up again, a big man with his head wrapped in cloth and holding a large spear and pointing towards us so the three of us hurried again and I was a bit left because I still couldn't even my tired legs would run and hide for a few days because of the Penac and crazy people who were here.

Fortunately, the pursuer was behind us and we went straight to our plan so we wouldn't get lost in our path.

Here I noticed that Katho Don noticed me having difficulty running so he turned around and positioned himself behind me just in case a mad big man with a spear attacked me. I felt Katho's little kindness. I don't know if it springs from inside him because his face is frowning and annoyed when he does these and he told me to hurry up old man. What he ventured was somewhat true but hurt my feelings a little.

We got to the Deltor Museum pretty quickly and were immediately opened by a strong push from Rion Hein.

We heard a very loud sound of I don't know if it was bats or rats and we were surprised at the oversized courtyard of the Deltor Museum, Katho Don immediately pushed us inside and suddenly the door closed.

I saw a lot of smoke running inside of the edge of all paintings and this very old vibrant energy would get a long fright if we are cowards but now I knew this is not an ordinary museum, because I heard this place is an anathema in centuries ago. When I was a kid my father shared his father would be here and never came back after he had a mission to search and gather this area that's why almost a lot of people say that this place is malediction.

We managed to escape the man holding the

spear-sword but I felt bad here in the place we

entered.